BLACK
FROM
THE
FUTURE

A COLLECTION OF
BLACK SPECULATIVE WRITING

EDITED BY
STEPHANIE ANDREA ALLEN & LAUREN CHERELLE

BLACK
FROM
THE
FUTURE

A COLLECTION OF
BLACK SPECULATIVE WRITING

PRESS

Clayton, NC

Printed in the United States of America

First Printing, 2019

Cover design: Lauren Curry

Cover photography: Joel Filipe, Jessica Felicio

Paperback ISBN-13: 978-0-578-50213-7

Library of Congress Control Number: 2019944283

BLF Press
PO Box 833
Clayton, NC 27528

www.blfpress.com

Contents

Caramelle 1864
Jewelle Gomez

for Sheridan LeFanu

I watched my father, Solomon, scan the road outside of our small house for a sign. It was always uncertain whether he was more relieved when he discovered one or when he did not. He often invoked the name of the Lord either way, but he sometimes appeared too exhausted to remember further prayers. He was a tall man, thinly built, who always looked as if he had important jobs to do. Watching for the sign was one of them.

He wiped his delicate, dark hand over the tight nap of hair that capped his head before turning to me. I looked away quickly, as I often did, pretending to study my lesson book on the table before me. Now, when I think of my father, it is those fleeting moments that bring his face to my mind most precisely. The look in his eyes—a mixture of anxiety, excitement, and love. Coiled inside of him was a fierceness that his wiry frame almost concealed, but not quite. And freedom was always his goal. He spoke of it to me and everyone who would listen so often that freedom became a tangible thing, a thing to taste like berry pie. And it became our name—Freeman—when we settled.

We'd come to live in Charlmont before my memory starts, but I do know it followed my mother's passing to the other side. We'd lived on the small farm for some years before I understood—our farm was a depot—a place where those, like my father and me, stopped on their way to freedom. No one ever actually said these words, but the succession of 'cousins' who stayed with us in the years before I turned 14 were innumerable. Each would be called by the same name depending on the age. Men were called Cousin Simon, women were Cousin Delia, and children were Cousins Henrietta or John. I think Father decided to use the same names so as not to tax my childish memory.

Sometimes, it became a source of a smile for Father and me. He'd look up, and say, "Wonder if we'll have a Cousin for dinner tonight?" And I'd answer, "Yes, please. May we have them with jam?"

It was the purest joy to hear my father laugh out loud; he usually parsed his responses and words as if he never wanted to be surprised into revealing something.

Later, I heard the stories of the life of slavery he'd left behind on the plantation. Mostly from the Cousins who 'visited.' One whose skin was drawn so tight by the scars of the lash she could hardly bend over. Another who walked with such a severe limp I wondered how he'd been able to cross the great distance from the world of slavery to our New England farm at all.

By the time I was fourteen, it ceased feeling like a secret game and I understood the stark terror the Cousins had endured to make the journey north. It was the same terror and grief that had driven my father to figure out to put on my mother's clothes and escape with me in his arms.

"We've got cousins tonight."

"With jam?"

He grinned and said, "Cousin Delia and Cousin Henrietta be here tonight."

With that I went to the area where I slept to be certain I'd not left a terrible mess. I was, by nature, quite neat; however, I was sometimes prone to leaving my pieces of paper about when I was studying my books. I believe I'd be a might less lonely if I could write things down. I didn't dwell on loneliness usually, but there it was, sitting at the foot of my bed.

I heard the buckboard on the road before Father did. His hearing was getting thinner each year, which he would never admit, of course. Mr. Leavitt, pale in the dim light thrown by the lantern at his side, helped Cousin Delia down first. She was tall and fair-skinned, almost as pale as Mr. Leavitt. She wore her head wrap drawn tight down across her brow, shadowing her eyes. She was very thin, not unexpected given the journey they'd taken. The flight from the south to the north was hardly a nutritious one.

Delia reached up to lift her daughter down before Mr. Leavitt could, and the sinewy strength of her arms and back were barely concealed by the dark cloak she wore. Cousin Henrietta was almost as tall as her mother and just as pale. She could have been 11 or 16. It was difficult to tell in the dim light. Mr. Leavitt handed my father a small satchel, barely said good night, and climbed back up on the seat of his buckboard. That was unusual; Mr. Leavitt's way was shy but regular. He'd come in to settle his charges, often have a cup of cider to be neighborly, and then promise to return with more 'victuals.'

That meant he'd return with the guide for the next aspect of our journey. Tonight he turned, looking exhausted as if he'd not slept in days. I suppose when he came on Sunday we'd hear more of what might be going on outside our little town.

"Goodnight to you, sir," Mr. Leavitt said.

We turned to our charges and offered a small snack.

"We kinda tired, suh. If you don't mind we'd like to...."

"I understand, Cousin. No tea?"

"Naw."

I couldn't see her eyes well, but they didn't look tired at all. Her voice didn't seem as weak as her words, but I couldn't tell; so I turned to her daughter. She stared back at me with coal black eyes that were full of fear. That made more sense than the sound of her mother's voice, so I took her hand and led her to the space she'd occupy until it was time for them to move north.

Once they were settled in Father rolled back his blanket so I could sleep in his bed in the narrow alcove, and then he slid the curtain across on the thick branch, which rested at the top of the wall. He checked the bolt across the door and settled on a pallet by the stove. I loved the sound of Father nestling into the wool-covered hay; it reminded me of the barn.

And then it was morning. Father was outside but there was no sound from my room.

Father said Cousin Delia had asked they not be disturbed, they might sleep through the day and as well as being exhausted she and her daughter suffered from an eye disorder that made bright light hard on them. I put a piece of ham bone in a pot at the back of the stove and then worked outside gathering greens and pulling in more hay for the barn. Father took the horse over to the Fahey farm to help with their tilling, and I tried not to listen at the door to my room. I wanted to truly meet Cousin Henrietta.

Near dusk, done with my chores around the farm, I ran water over my head like Father always did, and I loved the way it soaked my collar even though I knew Father would not be pleased. No one could resist the smell of my stew, so I pulled dishes out and set them on our small table. I decided to use our cloth napkins even though it wasn't Sunday. I'd have to wash them before the men came for their meeting but I didn't mind; I wanted the cousins to feel welcome.

Cousin Delia stood in the doorway. I'd seen many different colors of colored people since we'd had the visiting cousins, but something about this Delia was unlike anyone I'd ever met. Coolness rolled off of her like fog rising from the cranberry bog. I smiled, though, and asked if she wanted tea.

"Yes, that be nice…uh…?"

"Elisabeth," I provided. Father had given me mother's name after she passed.

Delia looked at me as if we were really related and said, "How fortunate."

I thought that was a confounding response, but people on the railroad often had an odd relationship to words, to space, to everything. It was like they were trying to understand the world when they had only been living in it underwater. Everything is familiar but distorted; nothing comes easily.

"Mama?"

Cousin Henrietta stood behind her mother. Her eyes were the same dark pools, but I could see a smile lurking there. This was my favorite thing: to learn who the children were before they were gone. Then for days I'd imagine the mysterious places they might have landed—New York or Canada. I always thought of them as having tea somewhere nice and sunny and cool.

The kettle came to a boil and I made tea for them both in our old, chipped pot, and decided to wait for Father to have mine. Before he returned Delia announced she wanted to go out for a walk. I told her Father would advise against it, and she sat back in her chair as if he'd actually spoken.

"Well then…" she said, indecision filling the air.

"Father will be home soon and we'll have supper."

They were silent. Henrietta smiled, though.

"I'm going out to the barn to set the hay for when Father comes back with the horse. You want to come?" I said to her.

"Oh yes, please."

Her mother almost said no but held back inside.

I took her hand and said, "Come along, Cousin Henrietta." I was relieved to be out of the house, which was filled up with her mother's anxiety. I didn't know if this was the natural state of mothers since I'd not known one, but it was a distinctly unpleasant feeling.

"My name is Caramelle."

"You mustn't say that."

"Well it is, and I don't like being called something else."

Once we were inside I shut the barn door like always and she looked startled.

"Why'd you do that?"

"You're supposed to shut the barn door so there's no coming and going."

Something about that made her laugh and laugh and then me too. We laughed until we fell down into the pile of hay and the chickens cackled around us. We lay there smiling at the beams and tackle hanging above us.

"I remember this place."

"How can you remember a place you've never been?" I asked.

"Through dreams, silly!" Caramelle laughed again, which took the edge off of her words.

She watched me wield the pitchfork as I tossed the hay over into the horse stall and smiled like it was the most charming entertainment.

"Where have you traveled from?" I knew I wasn't to ask, but I couldn't stop myself.

"I ain't supposed to say."

Then she looked at the closed door and nestled into the hay like she was in complete comfort.

"Maryland."

"Didn't they already pass emancipation? That's what the white men told Father!"

"Yes, but we had to get on the road any way."

"Oh?"

"I'll tell you the tale because I'm so tired from carrying it all by myself. Mama, she knows, but she don't talk. You can see that, can't ya?"

That was for sure. Cousin Delia hadn't spoken more than ten words in the ten hours she'd been in our house.

"A man, a friend of the massa, used to come all the time and bother me." Cousin Henrietta, I mean Caramelle's eyes got even darker as she spoke.

"He was always fearsome, cold. And he looked at folks like they weren't really there. One night he…he turned into something. He locked us in the room and he turned me into something."

"I don't understand."

"I can't explain exactly, but mother too. He did it to her too."

"What about your daddy? Didn't he…?"

"Massa were my daddy."

I stopped pitching the hay then and looked at the girl who was curled up before me. She was both innocent and old at the same time. I knew the cruelties that infected slave owners, but I hate that it had touched Caramelle.

"Do you want to see the secret place?" I asked. I might have to show it to them soon anyway, but this seemed a good time.

"See here."

I opened to gate to the stall and dug the pitchfork around under the hay until I found the seam in the wood floor. I pried until the hatch opened and revealed the trough we'd dug into the ground below. It was lined with hay and a blanket but was still not the most inviting place to bed down. We'd only used it once when a relentless bounty hunter had followed some cousins almost to our door. But that had been more than a year ago, and the news was that the war was almost over.

"Let's get in!" Caramelle said with excitement.

I tipped the hatch back and Caramelle dropped in like she'd been invited into a grand salon. I looked at the closed barn door and then slid down beside her in the hole. It could not have been more than four feet by six feet and was about four feet deep. I closed the hatch over us and a few sprigs of hay drifted down through the cracks.

Caramelle started to giggle and put her arm around me. She wriggled in close and whispered in my ear: "Can I tell you the rest?"

I couldn't imagine what more there would be.

"He tried to take me and mama from Massa Harriwell, that 'twere his name, but the misses didn't want to let us go since she loved how my mama could rub people's pain away."

I had, indeed, noticed the strength of her hands and the muscles that lined her arms last night. It seemed unusual for someone so slight.

"Well, he was determined and Massa Harriwell finally give us up, not for cheap though."

"Once we was on the road that man kept messing with me, and one night mama just got mad and killed him."

"Killed him?"

"Yeah. She pick up the small hatchet she keep in her things and took off his head. She said that was the only thing to do. But that meant we really had to run now. She said his people was gonna be mad and we had to get north."

The chill that surrounded her mother now also emanated from Caramelle. I hadn't noticed that before. Or maybe remembering the death of her tormentor had dropped her temperature in a fit of emotion.

"We been traveling ever since, trying to figure out how to live since he used to take care of that."

"Take care of what?"

"We better git, ain't your papa coming home soon?" Caramelle said abruptly.

"Yes," I said more confused than when the story was started. I understood about white men messing with girls. I understood about escaping and sometimes killing. The people who met with my Father tried to talk in low tones so I wouldn't hear about dying, but I did.

Caramelle and I pushed open the hatch together and climbed out, brushing straw from our clothes. I realized then that I wanted to give her something new to wear. Her own clothes were caked with mud and dark stains. I determined then to sew something for her.

It was a funny dinner we had when we all sat down. Father was almost jovial and I kept thinking it was because of Caramelle's mama. She had snuck out the house while we were in the barn. I could tell because she had brambles on her skirt, but her walk had done her good and she even laughed when Father told her stories.

We were up later than usual talking when she asked Father if she could rub his shoulders. He was startled then Caramelle said: "The missus really 'preciated mama's shoulder rub. You should, I'm telling you!"

Father laughed and said, "Well, with a recommendation like that from our little cousin, how can I say no?"

With that he sent me and Caramelle to bed and Cousin Delia rubbed my Father's shoulders with those strong hands of hers; hands that had wielded an ax and took a man's head off.

I didn't think I could sleep knowing that, but I barely lay down before it felt like it was morning.

Caramelle and her mama kept to the room in the morning. I went about my chores quietly and even did my studying early so I'd be free to enjoy Caramelle when she finally emerged. It did give me a chance to think about what kind of dress I'd be making. I'd asked Father and he agreed it would be a neighborly thing to do.

When she emerged, Caramelle was as eager as I to get back to our secret place where we both felt at home.

"Tell more about what you spoke of yesterday...learning to...."

"Mama don't want us talking about that."

"She didn't want me to know your name is Caramelle either."

I'd come to love the sound of her name. It reminded me of something soft and warm, even though her small body remained chilled as she curled around me under the floorboards in the horse stall.

A scent of coolness misted her skin, yet her dark eyes burned hot. Where she touched me I felt warm and something else. It was as if she were touching not just my skin but my blood and bones too. Like her mother's, Caramelle's hands were uncommonly strong. I was pleased at that because I always hated the idea that girls were weaker than boys.

I leaned in closer and absorbed the sensation of being held with the strength of Caramelle and barely heard her story because of the joy flowing through my body.

"I beg your pardon?"

"You silly thing!" Caramelle said, laughing. "You're not falling asleep are you?"

"No, not at all. Please go on."

"We met her on the road. We were ragged with hunger and exhaustion. Gilda just stepped out of the dark and fed us. She was tracking us and that ain't so easy because we move pretty near fast as a...well fast...."

"Can we run together sometime in the woods?"

"If mama says."

I didn't want to hold out hope since Caramelle's mother, despite her almost total silence, managed to convey a sense that she would not approve of much that Caramelle and I would want to do.

"So her and mama talked mostly quiet-like 'til mama said something and Gilda got real hard and scared me. But then her voice was soft again and I think she told mama things about how we could make it north without the slave catchers gettin' us. Then she rubbed my face, smiled, and leaned down to kiss me, but instead she whispered: 'You see trouble call me, you hear.' I think that's what she said anyway. That's when I ask my mama what her name was 'cause I wondered how I was gonna call her if I didn't know her name.

"I hadn't seen a smile like that since mama...since he changed mama. Then Gilda just disappeared like she'd come... into the dark." Caramelle stopped abruptly.

"Gracious! You think she was an escaped slave?"

"Uh…I don't think so. She walked like…I don't know… just different. And she talked different too. More like you. And she was wearing men's clothes! I knew she was a woman though, so did my mama."

I could see Caramelle was feeling sad so I didn't push her. Her mother probably didn't want her to feel so sad, and I supposed that's why she forbade her talking about these things.

The next day, Caramelle rose shortly before her mother as if she was as eager as I to enjoy each other's company. She almost caught me as I basted a piece of the fabric Father had brought home. He'd convinced me to make an apron, not a dress; he said our cousins wouldn't be staying long enough for such a project.

I'd just finished adding a bit of grosgrain ribbon I had left from a dress I'd made for myself, and all that remained was to hem the bottom. I slipped the almost completed gift under my own apron when Caramelle appeared in the doorway. Her eyes were bright.

"Come, let me redo your hair."

"Mama will do it."

"No, please let me."

I took down the brush from behind the one mirror we had hanging by the reading table and had Caramelle sit between my legs on the floor where I used to sit when Father combed my hair.

I brushed gently and redid each part neatly so it looked exactly as it had before. I don't know why, but just before I finished braiding, I leaned down and kissed the center part where the sweetness of her scalp showed through. I slipped a small piece of the left-over ribbon from the apron and tied the ends of the rows together at the base of her head making a tiny bow.

"Ohhh! I never had a bow before!" Caramelle said, touching the piece of fabric gently as if she could see it with her fingers.

"Look mama," Caramelle said. Without turning she'd clearly heard her mother step into the doorway. I was startled since there is usually a huge squeak in the board just before the door, which I had to deliberately avoid whenever I got up in the middle of the night if I didn't want to wake Father.

"I see."

Her mother's voice was the saddest sound. Caramelle jumped up and threw herself into her mother's arms.

My heart sunk at that sight because it was a vibrant reminder that Caramelle belonged to her mother and they would both be gone soon. I went to the stove to stoke the fire so the stew I had cooking would be done when Father arrived. I slipped the apron under the bedding and went back to the stove, keeping my back to the image of Caramelle and her mother, although I would always see it.

"Mama, we got to go move hay in the barn now."

"Miss Elisabeth don't need you underfoot while she doin' her work, child."

"Mama I help. You know I'm strong."

"Cousin Delia, I love having Car…Cousin Henrietta with me. Please?"

"Alright."

The sound of defeat again seemed to hang over her as she sank down into the chair where I'd been combing Caramelle's hair.

We tried not to hurry out to the barn, but our feet did not obey. Father would be home soon and we both knew we had little time left together. Mr. Leavitt would send someone to take them north any time now.

"Can we…"

I had the floorboard pried up and lowered myself before Caramelle could finish asking.

"You know why we got to go all the way to Canada?"

"The slave catcher?

"Naw, mama say since she killed that man his people is coming after us."

"The master?"

"Ain't him. It's the ones that change people like he did me and mama."

"I don't know what you mean."

"I can't say exactly, except we ain't like we used to be… the day light is hard on us and we have to…"

Here, she stopped and I almost wanted her to stay silent. Something in her voice made me afraid. Through the slats of the floor light filtered down to our hiding place, floating on the bits of hay. Her arms were tight against me and I wanted to feel her breath on my neck as she spoke.

"That hateful man took our lives. First, he was messing with me, which mama said was shameful. Then, he took our lives."

"What does that mean?"

"He…he made it so we have to drink blood to stay alive."

Caramelle said it in that childlike voice that I'd come to love, but the shock of it swept over me. She sensed it and held me closer.

"Please don't be afraid. I promise I won't hurt you."

"I never thought you would, Caramelle. I just don't understand what you're saying."

"There's some folks that…this is the way they live. Mostly they mean like the one who took us. Kind of like the massa but worse 'cause they don't die."

I wanted to laugh but I couldn't. Suddenly, I felt too big for the little space below the floorboards and Caramelle's arms were so tight around me I couldn't move.

"Miss Gilda told mama everything. That made her feel better for a while, but she's still really scared the others are coming after her. You ain't supposed to kill the one who…"

Caramelle stopped as if she couldn't bear to talk about it anymore, and I nestled in closer to assure her I wasn't afraid and because it felt so good to have her body close to mine.

"Want me to show you something? I promise it won't change you."

"Yes," I said, although the breath gathered in my chest and almost choked off the word. My heart pounded with both fear and anticipation.

Caramelle leaned up on one elbow and pressed her mouth to mine. It was gentle at first, and since I'd never had such a kiss my first response was to be startled. Caramelle held on to my shoulders and her lips were insistent on mine until she said:

"Yes?"

"Yes," I answered and her mouth became surprisingly warm. I returned her kiss and the warmth became a fire that I felt down to the bottom of my stomach and then beyond. I could barely breathe but was desperate to keep her mouth on mine. I moaned as her mouth slipped away from mine then to my cheek and down to my neck. Now her lips were hot on my skin. I could feel the stirring inside me that sometimes came when I had dreams and I wanted only that she not stop.

There was a small sharpness at my neck and then she kissed me again, and I felt as if I was falling into a hole—except I was already in a hole. Caramelle's lips were the only thing I understood at that moment. She was looking inside my mind or my heart, I could feel that. When she pulled back she looked me in the eye and said, "Now you'll always be a part of me just as you wanted."

My eyes were out of focus and I felt as if the horse that usually occupied the stall above was standing directly on me.

"Rest. You'll be fine in just a moment, I promise. I didn't take much."

"Much?"

"That was one of the things that Miss Gilda taught me and mama. That nasty man just like to kill folks, but Miss Gilda said we don't have to."

I slept then and awoke to Father calling my name. His voice had a slight tinge of anxiety and I realized it must have gotten late.

"We have to hurry. Father doesn't like me to play under here anymore."

Caramelle looked at me carefully as if to make sure I was not ill-affected by our secret moment.

"Now I'll always be with you," I said with a smile to reassure her. I did feel a little lightheaded but nothing else seemed out of order; except I could not stop smiling at Caramelle, or she at me.

"I'm sorry Father, we were just..."

Caramelle's mother snatched her from my side.

"Mama!" Caramelle protested.

"Elisabeth, you gave our cousin a scare. She didn't know where you were."

"I do apologize, Cousin Delia. We wandered off as I was telling cousin all my stories."

"You didn't fall asleep out there in those woods, did ya?" There was a hint of terror in Cousin Delia's voice.

"No, cousin. Time just got away from us. I apologize."

"There. All's well that ends well," Father said.

"William Shakespeare, 1604," I answered with more pride because Caramelle could witness my scholarship.

I could tell Father wasn't angry because he'd played our game: throwing titles and quotations from texts I'd been studying, and he beamed when I got it right.

"What's that?" Caramelle asked.

"Let's have our last supper together and Elisabeth, who loves to tell stories so much, will tell you all about William Shakespeare."

I was extremely sad and happy at the same time. I could already feel how I missed Caramelle, but I was also relieved that she would be taken north out of harm's way…slave catchers or the family of the evil man.

"I'll be sorry to see you leave us, cousins," Father said. His voice made me understand that he was as lonely in this life as I was.

"There's been a bit of activity lately so we're sorry for the delay. But, tomorrow evening you'll be on your way and safe and sound before you know it."

"Mama, I felt safe here."

"I know, gal, but you can see we ain't. And if we stay they won't be either."

"I believe Elisabeth has a little gift she made for you, cousin. We want you to always remember us."

I reluctantly pulled the apron from beneath the covers on Father's bed. It wasn't completely finished and worse, when it was done, I knew they were gone for sure.

"I just have a few more stitches and it's finished…if you want it…" Caramelle squealed with joy as she held the little apron to her heart. We sat talking about the road, what Father could tell them about the way to Canada; things he'd heard from Mr. Leavitt. I finished the hem, turned over the ends of the apron strings, and Caramelle tried it on. "I'm sorry there wasn't time to make you a new dress."

"Oh this is much better for traveling! And if I get a new dress I'll make sure it matches this pretty color."

For the first time, Caramelle's mother's face was washed with a full and brilliant smile.

The soft knock on our door startled us all, as if it had been the crack of a cannon ball. The smile on Cousin Delia's face slid away and was replaced with a look of terror and then a fierceness I'd never seen. A visitor at this hour was rare unless there was some trouble, and the conductor wasn't due until tomorrow.

"Mr. Freeman?"

Father was surprised to hear his name; everyone in town just called him by his Christian name, except the Quakers who called everyone mister and miss. He opened the door more puzzled than afraid. A remarkable woman stood there in men's breeches and jacket with a hat in her hand. At first, I thought she was white; her skin was fair and almost translucent, much like Cousin Delia's but even more so. Yet around the edges I could see an almost bronze tone beneath her skin that told me she was a mulatto. And I could tell who it was by the catch of Caramelle's breath.

"Mr. Freeman, I apologize for the lateness of the hour, but may I come in?"

"Of course," Father said before Cousin Delia could say anything, although it was clear she had intended to protest.

"Ah, my cousins...good."

"May I ask..."

"Of course, again I apologize, Mr. Freeman, for interrupting your final evening, but it's impossible for them to stay here another minute."

I rushed to Caramelle's side and grabbed her hand. She clutched my little apron in her other hand as if it was gold.

"What do you want with us?" Cousin Delia sputtered.

"I want only to protect you. You know they are after you."

"Slave catchers...close?" Father was immediately suspicious. However, it was sorely uncommon for us to see many other colored people, especially a woman alone dressed as a man. We both had the impulse to put more wood in the stove and spend the night exchanging stories.

"Worse," she answered quickly.

"Madam," my father said sternly, "I assure there is no worse than a slave catcher."

"There is a bounty on their heads and the return of their bodies would be just as rewarding." Cousin Delia flinched as the words fell on her.

"Bounty? Why?"

"I'm afraid we don't have time for the full story. Cousin, tell them it is true so we may make our way before it's too late. Or, do you wish to see the blood of your hosts shed as well?"

I started to cry then because I couldn't bear to be separated from Caramelle, and I hoped for the briefest moment they might take me with them. Caramelle straightened beside me.

"Elisabeth, please stop cryin'. Mama knows we got to go with Miss Gilda."

"You know each other then?" Father was a bit relieved although still puzzled.

"I hate leavin' you, Elisabeth, but she right." Caramelle's voice was sweet but firm as if she knew she had to make the decision for her mother who was paralyzed with fear.

"But where will you go? I..." The words evaporated before I could say them. Not knowing where Caramelle would be seemed like a life much too bleak to comprehend.

"Dear Elisabeth, you really are true aren't you," the woman Gilda said to me and smiled her sincerity. "You mustn't be sad. I've a wonderful place for our cousins and it's perfect! Do you know why?"

"No." I tried to stop sniffling and be as grown up as my dear friend to whom I was still clinging.

"Well, it's perfect because it has the same name as she does. So deep in your heart you'll always know where she is."

"Can we see each other again?" I asked. My confusion was apparent.

"That is possible." Here Miss Gilda also looked sad. "If so it will not be for a long time. But, you mustn't worry. Are you ready?" She turned to Cousin Delia who was locked inside her fear. "Even Caramelle has learned more quickly than you!" Miss Gilda's voice remained soft but carried a hard edge that was chilling. "Take only what you need and leave something in exchange. You will be able to live and not like the others. You must believe me."

Cousin Delia's stillness broke and she turned to take up her cloak.

"We'll make a wide circle, leading away from this farm and then head north. Once we're in another territory you'll be safe."

"How can you be sure?" Father asked, not really clear what he was asking.

"I've seen this before. The bounty will be void as long as they don't return to this territory."

"All right cousins. Let me pack up some of that meat that was in the stew and the rest of the bread."

"That won't be necessary," Miss Gilda said, adding quickly, "I've nourishment hidden along the route."

"You've been a true cousin, Mr. Freeman," Cousin Delia finally said. "We thank you and Miss Elisabeth for your kindness."

Caramelle threw her arms around my neck and kissed me where she had taken my blood and whispered: "I left something in exchange."

Miss Gilda watched us closely all the while speaking in a bare whisper that was almost mesmerizing.

"No one should follow. And if anyone asks you will have no recollection of our whereabouts. I've already communicated with Mr. Leavitt, so there's no need to speak with him. All's well that ends well, eh?" With that she smiled at me and put her arm around Cousins Delia and Caramelle, sweeping them out the door beside her.

The Night Has No Eyes
Kivel Carson

They came at night. And brought with them the trauma and fear of all the babies ripped from their mothers' arms, beings made less than human in the face of violence and humiliation, brightness turned to darkness and hurt. They came as the embodiment of all that unspent pain, and refused to die, made invincible by the same willful instinct that makes a dying man kick his feet in a last death rattle.

I can't explain it, but when I first saw them, I thought of chickens— the ordinary bird domesticated for slaughter and producing eggs that would never mature to a life. How they come home to roost. What they look like with their heads tilted to the side when their necks are broken. Their blood in the old hoodoo ways that conjured the impossible. The Sankofa bird on my rib, and my auntie's voice when she asked why I tattooed a chicken on my body.

I had a tightness in my chest as I moved through the night on the shadowy road where my tire blew. I knew where I was. There were signifiers that stood high as warnings— confederate flags that dotted lawns, place names celebrating a glorious past and the future it produced, the absence of us. I walked alone, an imposing dark figure in the moonlight, shrouded by gray cotton that revealed only the shadow of my face and the locs spilling out of it. An unknown could emerge from the tall trees lining the highway and test the strength of the outstretched branches with my weight. Death could sit high behind head-lights, barreling toward me from the nothingness. Flashes of red and blue could illuminate the night and splash over me, bury me where I stood. Fear is a funny thing, who feels it and who yields its power. I should've felt relief to see the glow of light in the distance, a sign of life, but I only felt more dread. Life, perhaps, but not life for me. Only more danger, waiting.

Their eyes fell heavy on me when the dangling bell on the screen door tolled to announce my presence. It's incredible to be pierced with eyes that can never quite meet your own, and to be watched without really being seen. Adrenaline flushed my bloodstream as hairs stood up on my skin and I clenched my jaw, deadened my eyes, readied my mask. Red splotched across their faces and necks and I almost felt the heat from where I stood. One behind the counter with a wall of cigarettes lining the backdrop like wallpaper. Two seated to the left with Styrofoam takeout plates. A fourth further in the corner with a newspaper and tall bottle of beer. My eyes scanned and met the clerk's.

"My car got a flat and I have no service, I just need to use the phone," I said.

"Phone's for paying customers," he said back, folding his arms. I saw him assessing my form, trying to find a box to place me in, looking for hairs on my chin or a sign of feminin-ity beneath my hoodie. I tossed a pack of gum on the counter and pulled my credit card from my pocket.

"Five dollar minimum for cards, and I'll have to see some ID."

"I have to pay five dollars to use the phone, and show ID to spend five dollars?"

"Or you can *not* use the phone and walk back to your flat tire, sir."

My blood boiled, but I was frozen by the voice of my mother telling me to be careful as the door slammed behind me. At 7 going to ride my bike. At 12 going to explore the park in my neighborhood. At 16 going to a pool party with my friends across town. At 17 walking to the store down the street in the rain to buy snacks. At 22 driving the empty road back to campus after a long weekend. I swallowed the rage making a lump in my throat and turned to peruse the closest aisle for $5 worth of junk food.

The bell on the door ratted again and I prepared for the confrontation— the buddy they called to teach me a lesson, the cop with his gun drawn, the white woman I would make feel unsafe. Instead, everything went quiet. Even the screams were quiet at first, muffled by the white noise between my own ears, until they pierced through and flooded the entire place. I dropped to my knees behind a shelf and took cover. There was a throaty grumbling spliced between the screams and sounds of flesh being thrashed and pulled from bone. I sucked air deep in my lungs and whispered prayers through the exhales. I peeked around the endcap and couldn't process what my eyes were reading. There was an image with no context, so I just thought of chickens, and how they come home to roost, and what that even means, two generations removed from the farm.

There had been reports of attacks, in the night, by animals, deranged addicts, or a Satanist cult. Nothing verified, nothing concrete linking the sporadic deaths that seemed to have started near the eastern North Carolina-Virginia line and thinly dotted the map in a southwestern swing. There were only carnage and questions and fear. Fear for others who didn't have so many realities to fear daily, and had the privilege of hypothetical fears to keep them awake instead.

When I saw their black bodies, covered in a white ash that falls over the elders before they pass on, I felt a strange peace that I took to be resignation. I rested the back of my head against the shelf and sat with the calm, waiting for death. Her sudden presence above me broke through the haze. Another dark body, vibrant with life, falling curls about her head and shoulders, a deep brown aura. She floated in a calmness, too, awestruck, unable to breathe while watching from the bathroom doorway. I pulled her by her hand into a crouch beside me and covered my lips with a finger. I heard the swishing that fabric makes when it moves through the air and felt a coldness creep over me. She gripped my hand, or maybe I was gripping hers. A stout woman with a resolute face, and a wrap snugly tied around her head like a high cotton crown, rounded the corner and stared down at us. A rusting rifle hung from her shoulder in a sling. No one breathed. Her hollow, cloudy eyes fixed on me and I felt my entire body get warm and electric, transfixed by the power. It felt like I would levitate but for the other woman's hand on mine, grounding me. It all must have happened in only a moment, then the figure was gone, along with the others like her and the gnashing and screams. We remained. The silence returned.

There was blood and flesh and bone everywhere, painted on the walls and floors. It hollowed me out, but a drive inside me took over.

"Is your car outside?"

She nodded.

"We have to get out of here."

She nodded again, still silent, as we rushed through the door and heard the bell for the last time. A siren was faint in the distance.

"I had a flat about a mile back. Can—"

"Get in," she said.

Her pale knuckles gripped the steering wheel as she stared straight ahead in a daze. She drove down the road in the opposite direction of my car, but neither of us could speak or process at the moment. I let the dotted yellow lines of the road and the bass and synth of the mix playing through her speakers hypnotize me.

"Zora."

At some point, my voice broke through the silence in a deep, smooth tone that didn't match the rapid thumping in my chest.

"Huh?" she replied, descending from her fog.

"I'm Zora."

"Simone," she said faintly. "I just stopped to use the bathroom, and..." She shook her head in disbelief.

"That happened, right? There's blood on my shoe," I said.

She glanced at me, as if to make sure I was real.

"You had a flat?" she asked. "I heard you, but I didn't hear you. I just started driving."

"It's cool, I appreciate you taking on a stowaway."

"Do you have a spare?"

"Yeah, it was low too."

"I have one that should be good, and you can just get it back to me when you get your tire straight," she said. "Where am I going?"

"You can just hit 561 and it'll take you back around."

She looked over at me again and back to the road.

"You have no idea where that is, do you?" I asked.

"Not at all."

"I could tell by your voice you weren't from around here," I said, trying to distract myself from the reality of what just happened. "Where are you from?"

"Gary, Indiana."

"Like Michael Jackson?"

"Kind of like Michael Jackson," she said with a smile. "Like here, but colder, and fewer country ass bugs."

"Hang a right," I said, pointing at a road ahead. "How did you end up down here?"

"Each One Teach One."

"You're a teacher? You don't look like a teacher. You have a bull ring."

Her laugh showed nearly all of her teeth. "What do I look like?"

"Some kind of edgy photographer. Or a lost grad student."

She laughed harder, until it made me laugh. And then there were tears on her cheek. "What the fuck just happened?" she whispered. Her tone was sober again. "What were they?"

"I don't know," I said, letting the reality push its way back in.

"They were people, right? They were us," she continued, still looking for words. "And the way she looked at us, like she knew us. I felt something. I just need someone else to tell me they saw what they were."

"Who they were," I mumbled. "Yeah, I saw it too."

I had seen them before, in their flowing linens, in films about the pre-war south, dotting cotton fields like ornaments, and in old sepia photos with fraught looks, that only told the half of it. But, I had never seen them as they were, as alive as me, or something like it, now.

"And they didn't touch us," she said wrinkling her forehead. "Only them."

"561's just up here." The road curved. "Take this right." I paused for a moment. "My great grandmother used to talk about Zonbis," I said, remembering. "She was Gullah Geechie and old, and people just thought she was talking. But, she talked about them like a prophecy, like other people talk about Jesus coming back. They weren't *The Walking Dead* kind. 'ZON-bee' is how she would call them with her thick accent. She said their souls couldn't rest, they couldn't return home until they finished some purpose, and Samedi could come and bring their peace, lead them back. They're conjured by the ones that know, when it's time, the ones who have the special sight. When she was dying, she used to chant in this whisper that scared me when I was young. And my grandma did the same thing before she died. My mom told me it wasn't just chanting, it was a conjuring, to give peace to the ones left behind, and curse the ones who cursed us in life."

The road grew darker as we got closer to my car.

"But you know, just old stories," I said.

"Your grandmother was from here?"

"*South* Carolina. But, I'm from here, born and raised. And returned."

"What brought you back?"

"A lot, but I'm still figuring that out... Samedi, maybe," I continued with a laugh. "I came back when my grandma was dying, and I just saw the need. I saw what was happening in my community and what the kids were going through here, and I remembered being that kid, and I just couldn't leave it how I found it. I run a little community garden for the kids now, and teach them art and culture through the land. And, I remodel houses during the day to pay the bills— hanging dry wall, adding fixtures, painting inside and out."

"How did you know this is what you were supposed to be doing?"

"My spirit or gut or whatever you want to call it didn't give me a choice. It didn't let me rest or eat or see anything else until I listened."

"Teaching here was like that for me. I was never supposed to end up here. It wasn't in any of my plans. But, somehow I had to."

The road opened up as we came closer to the point where we started.

"My car's up here on the left, just after the tree line starts," I said.

A flickering orange glow dimly backlit the trees ahead.

"Wait, slow down." I squinted my eyes and tried to make out what was in the distance.

"You see it too?" she asked. "What is that?"

"I think something's on fire back there."

She let down her window to smell for smoke, and crept slowly along the road. There was a low melodic moan.

"Do you hear that?" I asked. "I *know* that sound. I can't explain it."

She pulled off the road and parked in the grass overlooking a clearing in the trees.

We both got out without a word, both knowing better.

"Do you think it's a cross burning?" she whispered.

The light gleamed more brightly and the grumbling sound turned to a chant. She climbed onto the hood of her car, then the roof. I followed instinctively, as if my own feet didn't carry me. My eyes widened and my breath caught in my lungs. I collapsed into a seat, with my feet dangling over the side of the car. She eased down beside me in silence.

The black figures moved around a central glowing fire, like they were floating, falling lightly on their feet. Their cotton clothes spun with them like linens blowing in the wind on a clothesline. They chanted the song in throaty grumbles, a harrowing melancholy spiritual mixed with the joy of release. Tears streamed down both of our faces as we watched them dance in the firelight, unable to contain ourselves. I don't know how long we were there, suspended in the almost ethereal trance, watching. We watched until their fire went out and they disappeared into the trees.

I drove home in the dead of night with flashes of the woman with the rifle slung over her shoulder in my head, and Simone, and the bodies moving around the fire. That night, I couldn't sleep, but I dreamt of murky water, and freedom.

I was standing in my bedroom in the darkness, sipping a cup of hot tea, smoking papers, peering into the darkness. Something beyond my door pulled at my legs and played tricks on my eyes, making someone move before me and beckon me with an unseen finger. My feet moved across the cool grass to the edge of water, buried deep in the woods. There was calmness over it, a stagnant film, until a body thrust from beneath and moved toward me on the bank. It was the woman from the store, alive and full of color, in her own time, climbing from the water with the rifle on her back. Bodies sprung up behind her from the swamp, water dripping from their heads and clothes. I backed away from the water as they marched forward, until the woman stood in front of me toe to toe with her hand outstretched, and there was nowhere left to retreat. She pointed with a sharp, bony index finger, grazed it against my chest, and plunged it into my heart. I fell to my knees in a scream. But, it wasn't pain, more like a declaration. A soldier being marked for battle.

When I sprung up from my bed, gasping for air, I was soaked in sweat. And I thought of chickens. What they sound like when they crow in the morning in the garden to begin the day, and how they come home to roost, and their blood spilled in the old hoodoo rituals to conjure the impossible.

The Seam Ripper
Almah LaVon Rice

Pinned in place, riveted by the rip in my mother's body.

-- did...did it? *Did it work?*

Lila rises with a rustle and perches on one of the beeping machines. Doesn't answer, and then shakes her head to shush me. Time is featherweight now, any breath of doubt could blow this whole thing away.

But still.

-- is it happening? I ask.

I try to gather myself.

And then, a head crowning. My head! There I am, nothing but a wailbody, a squabble of flesh. But my skin is cloudy, barely pale brown, compared to my mother's nightblue.

I look to see how Mother is looking at me. Do we latch eyes? *Does she hold?* Does she hold me?

From the hole of my mother instead of an umbilical cord there are red threads trailing, dangling. Already snipped.

* * *

I had just finished fussing with the nasturtiums and put the vase down hard on the kitchen table. Lila opened her beak as if to speak, and then closed it. What could she say? My heart was broken again, but she didn't do the breaking.

This kitchen was yolk yellow, cheery with all the colorful plates and paintings from Lila's annual trips back home to Mexico. But there seemed to be a shadow stored in every pot.

   -- I wish I was enough, Lila said, as if reading my thoughts.
   -- Baby, you are.
   -- Taylore, but...

Instead of trying to continue with the lie, she looked downward and pulled on the piping of her dress. Lila should have been more than enough. My hummingbird wife, with just a drop of human in her DNA. Why she endured a moody girl like me, who turns from dull silver to stony gray when she's upset (which is often, and right now), while Lila is all plume and dazzle, all the time. The only evidence that I have a bird of paradise plant for a father is my crow-black spiky hair, which only retained his saffron and purple coloring at the very tips. I never even got to meet him. But there is no trace of my time in my mother's body--I have none of my mother's ultramarine skin, or her generous lips, or 20-foot height.

And that is exactly the problem. All my life I have caught my mother waiting and chanting by the shore. She would be watching the horizon, willing a better girlchild to surface. She would call to the seam of sky that holds her real daughter from her. Waiting and watching, watching and waiting, it's when the sun unstitches itself from the horizon that she thinks, *Maybe now, maybe her.* But no she-creature crawled from the water to my mother's feet; the ocean kept its daughters-of-pearl.

I would hide in the marram grass, watching her, until it got dark. Then I would run home so I could get there before she did. I would brush my feet until they almost bled to make sure they were free of sand. If she knew I kept a co-vigil for my sister, my substitute, she never let on. For once I'm thankful that my mother didn't hug or get close to me on those nights; if she had, she might have caught the smell of her own disappointment in my hair.

* * *

I must have looked lost, because Lila reached across the table for my hands.

-- What can I do? she asked finally.

-- What you got? I snort. Can you change the past? Turn back time?

She looked thoughtful, cocking her head in that cute hummingbird way of hers. I grinned, waiting for her to smile back at my joke.

-- You know I migrate every year, right? she said instead.

-- Of course.

-- I mean, your scientists don't really get us. Some of us fly 49,000,000 body lengths when we travel.

My Lila always had a gem-sharp memory. Must be all the sugar. I slid another glass of tree sap in her direction.

But she doesn't make a move to eat it, in the quick, little bites, like she usually does. Now it was my turn to cock my head.

-- Okay, and….? I began.

-- Well, going 49,000,000 body lengths is quite miraculous, wouldn't you say? You see what I eat, right? Flan, baklava—that's all I need to get on the road!

-- I don't think I'm following you, I quip.

-- Tay, what I'm trying to say is that going back to change things isn't a matter of time, it's a matter of calories.

-- Wait, what?
She waited for it to sink in. She was always too sweet to say it out loud, but I know she thinks humans—even one with a flower for a father—are adorable but kinda slow.

-- Hummingbirds c-can time travel? I sputtered.

-- The old hummingbirds say we can. Say we can fly all the way to heaven to carry your people's messages to the High Blue Gods. I've never done it, though. I'm willing to try... for you.

My mind spun. Or maybe I did have nothing but a muddy, slow river up there. I knew that if anyone could time-travel, it would be Lila. I've seen her embroider the air, and then dive-bomb the neighborhood cats just to make them jump and wonder, *where did she come from*? Not to mention the fact that, because she couldn't eat pecan pie and sleep at the same time, she had to practically die every night to conserve energy. She descended into a kind of coma, as close to death as a living being could possibly be. I would curl my body around hers to keep her warm, and in the morning, I would hold her while she told me about her dreams through that underworld.

-- Lila, I don't even know what to say.

She regarded me gravely.

-- Say that you know what this means, Tay. That it means that if I mess up, if I make a hole in the wrong place, your whole life could unravel. W-what if we never met, because the pattern got jumbled? She gets teary, voice breaking.

-- I know you can do this, baby. You have all those grand-mothers back home, you can ask them.

But I was not confident as much as I was desperate. Once I knew that changing the past was remotely possible, I knew we had to try. I had to try. I didn't really stop to really consider that I could lose Lila, that I could lose everything. Even if I had, I don't know if I would have chosen differently. When the option of time-tinkering arose, I didn't think of stopping the advent of agriculture, and thus the city-state, and thus the Industrial Revolution, and thus the overrun of people and their stuff. Climate change. I didn't think of erasing the Middle Passage. Genocide. I only thought, *Maybe I can figure out when my mother stopped loving me.*

* * *

I had to call her Mother. She would pop you in the mouth if you slipped and said *Mama* or *Mommy*. She claimed that because, growing up in Jim Crow Georgia, a woman as big and dark as her would get Mammy'd in a minute—and Mother didn't remind her of any of that. I think it was because Mother is stately and white and columnar. A pillar that holds up the roof to keep her Taylore—never Tay—dry. But a pillar does not rock, is cool to the touch.

-- You're making me hot, she would complain, pushing me away when I tried to hug her. *Mama* stunk of sweat and sticky child-palms on the neck.

To keep me warm, she made me patchwork quilts. I still have one of them: squares with pigtailed black dolls sewn on them. The dolls are wearing dresses made of the scraps of my dresses. After all these years they still gaze back at me with inscrutable painted smiles, stuck on the frieze of her word-less love.

* * *

So it begins. Lila laid tres leches at her ancestor altars. She flew back to Mexico to ask relatives so old that she knew they wouldn't be alive when she returned next fall. She took her notebook with her during her nightly torpor, so that she could jot down any clues from the underworld. She studied and she studied.

Eventually, her nighttime suspension between life and death spread to day. I would cut her a slice of her key lime pie, and she would fall dead-asleep before I could even get it on her plate. When she woke, she would tell me that she had been surveying the terrain of time just like she did the landscape during her yearly migrations. She wanted to memorize every dip, every turn, twist of the land below before attempting to take me with her.

* * *

I dream of a deer mother. She is looking at herself in the mirror. She threads turquoise flowers through her antlers, which are also plaits piled on top of her head. I look at my-self in the mirror; when I go to fix my own hair, I see the deer mother doing the same. How could I be me in flesh, and then another when I look at my reflection? To find out, I go to touch the mirror, to touch my Mother's face. She jumps back as if burned. The mirror goes dark.

* * *

I wake up in a panic. How could I have been orphaned in my sleep?

* * *

I dream that I am walking up winding marble steps. Around and around I go, as the steps are wound around an endless tree. When I finally reach the landing, I jump. Part of me makes it to the landing, while some of me remains on the step. I look back at myself, and I am even paler than usual, like the light gray I was when I was a small child. We smile at each other. It's happening.

* * *

I am less pleased with the progress when I'm awake, though. Lila is able to go back as far as my teen years, but still can't quite figure out how to carry me there as well. At least we learn my mother didn't stop loving me when I came out to her at 14. So no, that's not when I lost her, but it sure didn't help.

Lila studied even harder. She put down more offerings for the ancestors—pollen, insects, the purest sugar water. So she goes further back, back, back. Without me. But I have to go to see for myself, and to shuffle the seconds, the minutes, the hours myself. By the time Lila grabs a glimpse of five year-old me in a park, I am despairing. I have to be able to time-travel, too. When I can't—well, like Penelope, I am undone every evening.

* * *

When I hurt myself playing, Mother told me that scar fairies would come to me at night and sew me up in my sleep. Perhaps this was meant to be comforting, but not to the nervous half bloom-half child that I was. After falling off my bike and skinning my knee, I worried. I stayed awake all night. What if I woke up while the scar fairies were operating on me, scaring me to death?

I never saw a single scar fairy. Yet during one of my aunt's overnight visits, she said that she caught an angel leaving the dining room.

-- I only saw the hem of the angel's dress, she explained. Oh, and the frizzy hair. Did you know angels don't comb their hair?

* * *

In the end, it was a hem I grabbed to time-unravel. Like a sneeze that's a butterfly in the nose, close to flitting away—I woke in the morning to a dream almost-remembered. I get out of bed and stand up, as if that will help me recall. What was that dream? It was so vivid, and fading already.

And Lila's not in bed. Or in the bathroom getting ready for the day. The dream starts flooding back, one ghostly image at a time. Nothing's clear yet. Then Lila suddenly appears in the doorway, but doesn't look at me. I turn to see what she is looking at, behind me. Where our bed would have been, there's Mother, at least four decades ago, on a hospital bed. She's on her back, straining and pushing. Her impossibly long legs in stirrups. Doctor, nurse, and a woman I can't place, with a crown of orange and violet hair sticking straight up.

The doctor leaves, and then somehow the nurse fades as well. Just Mother and me roiling in her belly. And this woman I don't know, close to Mother, wiping her brow.

Lila looks at me and something in her eyes makes me look at the stranger again.

-- That's your mother's first and only love, she offers, but I already know. It's so clear to me now.

My mother loved another woman, a woman she loved so hard that I ended up looking a bit like her, not my father. Which ended up costing me--I could already see this coming--when this woman left Mother.

So this is who Mother was looking for on the beach.

This is where Lila lifts the seam ripper. Will this be where I am not even born? Or Lila undoes their love affair, so I come out looking like Mother herself, and so more lovable?

I hold my breath.

I take my first breath:
Mama.

Exodus

Lauren Cherelle

Cam watched the sky from the backseat of Meko's messy sedan. Every few moments, she'd glance down at Passage. It was nearly impossible to ignore how beautiful the place had become. The lush lawn and stone building didn't beg for signage or outdoor décor.

"Now?" Meko asked. He reached across the console for the bag in Aija's lap.

Aija flicked his hand. "Fall back."

Cam clenched her teeth, annoyed with Meko's impatience and sticky seats. "Not until the drones pass," she said.

"They have."

"Only one," Cam reminded him.

"Just pay attention," Aija said.

Police drones were often hard to spot and undetectable by sound. In time, however, the drones would shift in a direction that refracted the sunlight just enough to reveal their proximity.

Within minutes, Cam caught a glimpse of a small aircraft drifting away from Passage. "Now!"

Meko darted from the driver's seat and crossed the two-lane road, leaving Cam and Aija in his wake. Aija looked over with a smile and wink, her eyes afire with eagerness as she pranced along the pavement. "You ready?"

"No doubt," Cam said. She parted ways with Aija and buried her muddled thoughts. Truth was, she couldn't turn back now. It was too late.

Cam pushed her way into the frenzied crowd to the center of the grounds. Although they had rehearsed their roles and crafted a solid getaway plan, Cam couldn't lull her racing heartbeat. She gripped her backpack and settled behind the front line, nestled among older women with picket signs. "Turn back," they screamed. "Turn back. It's not too late!"

Cam was short and mostly petite, which made it easy to fade into the protest. And depending on what she chanted, or where she stood, she could blend with any of the regulars— the college students, the grieving parents, the relentless evangelists, the pro-life mommas, the right-wing activists. The naturalists were the exception. These were an assorted group of people that occupied the east side of the walkway, outnumbering the larger crowd. They wrapped their bodies in various textures of white, bare of signs and bullhorns. They equipped themselves with only the influence of their presence and voices.

Cam adjusted her cap and peered beyond the pro-lifers' picket signs. She sort of liked their hippie approach; they refused to carry digital boards or virtual gear. The classic style complemented their ferocity. "Choose life!" the women yelled at the approaching cluster of people. The group of seven walked closely, eyes glued to Passage, as if they couldn't hear the booming chants.

"It's okay to wait!" and "Don't give up!" were thrust at their faces. The incessant shouts clashed with the naturalist's gentle call: "Choose us."

One of the approaching women clutched the escort's arm, his lime safety vest eclipsing her face. Cam stole a moment to search for likenesses of herself. Occasionally, she shared an accidental glance with another brown girl with generous features passing through the deafening crowd. It stung to see faces akin to her mother's or sister's, her father's or uncle's, as they stumbled to the Passage entrance. Lately, she didn't remember exactly why she was fighting against these people. Was this still the best way to rupture the system?

And she wondered whether her presence mattered anymore. Cam dropped her head and cleared her thoughts. This wasn't the time or place to question her motives or actions. The plan was set, and the risks were justifiable. She unlatched her backpack and braced herself for Ajia's arrival.

Cam pressed through the pro-lifers and screamed, "Life is a gift." She stood on the frontline holding her backpack in one hand, the other hand pointed at those entering Passage to transition.

Transition to where— Cam wasn't sure. And neither was Aija or Meko or anyone else for that matter. Were people transitioning to a fresh start? An alternative existence? No one could define the plane beyond death, but the unknown of the other side didn't stop person after person after person from transitioning to that nameless place. A lot of people had opted for single bullets. Sharp blades. Strong ropes. High bridges. Other people wanted the assistance of Passage.

"Who pays to die?" a man spat. "Damn this capitalist bullshit!" His fury inflamed the crowd. Cam dug her sneakers into the lawn and leaned against the surge of people. Legally, the demonstrators couldn't break the line and spill onto the walkway. They had the right to flood the Passage campus, but the entranceways were off limits. Cam kept watch as the frontline struggled to maintain the barrier.

Cam spotted Aija and immediately opened her backpack. She waited until Aija and her male escort were only a few steps away before breaking the seal on a pack of firecrackers and tossing the igniting bundle onto the pebble walkway. The first round of casings exploded on landing, shifting Aija into second gear.

Aija dropped a can of red smoke into the chaos of footfalls and shoved her way through the rush of people. For a moment, Cam lost her balance in the swarm of bodies. She planted her feet on the pathway and touched off another round of firecrackers. The red cloud thickened as Aija and Meko scattered six-ounce cans across the lawn to intensify their ambush.

Cam retrieved a white shawl from her bag to cover her head and shoulders. She ran away from Passage in a horde of naturalists. When they reached the thoroughfare, she slowed to a stroll to catch her breath. Ahead, she noticed a naturalist clinging to a man in non-white garb, a man that had intended to enter Passage. Surely, the naturalists were headed toward a clandestine location, where they'd provide him a free, peaceful, natural death. She'd heard that naturalists used some liquid concoction of poisons. Cam ditched the group and the eerie feeling that had crept up her skin. She couldn't keep trailing down the sidewalk behind a man that — without a doubt— was experiencing his last moments of life. She ducked behind an industrial building to stuff the shawl into her bag.

Cam moved west at a brisk pace to avoid the suspicions of lingering drones or naturalists. At this point, Meko should have been in his car and nearing the expressway. Cam and Aija had agreed to travel by foot to the Broad Avenue station. Cam sought her phone to contact Aija and ensure she'd gotten away without injury. "Damn," Cam whispered. She had forgotten that her jeans pockets were empty. By law, Memphians waived recording privileges and privacy rights at mass demonstrations, which granted police drones free reign to upload social posts, virtual contacts, and tracking data from devices. So, rules forbade the crews from protesting with technology. Cam was alone and vigilant of those who could have remembered her face and ratted ahead of the train stop. But, if her crew could reach the warehouse— no arrests or casualties— she'd take a deep breath and lower her guard.

* * *

The warehouse teemed with energy and recounts of the morning's events. Cam and Aija found Meko twirling his sprouting locs while sitting with a group of friends. Aija thumped his hand. "You could have saved us a seat."

"It was full when I got here."

Here was a big structure on the edge of downtown with a sizeable interior cross and no interior walls. The Sunday school rooms and vestibule and choir stand and pews had been gutted or tossed years earlier. And the pulpit had been stripped to a foot-high platform. What remained was an open, collective space for community meetings.

Years ago, the platform was center stage for a handful of local, big-wig preachers and esteemed community activists. They would sit in a single row of folding chairs, surrounded by deacons, elders, and business owners. Together, they upheld a common sentiment: "We don't need some white scientist telling God's people what we already know. We've *all-ways* known what comes next," a pastor stressed. "We've been sharing the good news of everlasting life since He rose again."

"Preach!" the people sang.

"We've *all-ready* confessed our sins and accepted Christ as our Savior. We know that heaven lies ahead. And when I get there, *glo-ry*," the man crooned. "Can I get a witness?"

Cam had spent many days in those hard metal seats, resting her hand on her father's arm. A seven-year-old couldn't fight against sleepiness during those long, verbose meetings. The overarching message, however, never fell short of her young ears. With each visit, and each passing month, droves of Black families were reminded to choose life.

Much had changed in the last ten years. Those preachers had never imagined they'd lose the spiritual battle to a lone scientist. News of this man's discovery—and more importantly, his evidence— had spread like wildfire. For the first time, ever, the world knew, definitively, that death wasn't the end. That afterlife was real. And millions of people, from every continent, were electing to end their lives and "go forward."

At some point, the community meetings didn't dwell on the gift of life, and the united attitude deteriorated. Viewpoints shifted when a well-respected activist took the mic and challenged people to consider the bigger picture. "Chattel slavery. Jim Crow. Mass incarceration. Infectious disease. Poverty and drugs and war. The Ten-Year Collapse. *No-thing* has stopped our people!" She turned to the remaining preachers. "Damn your Jesus, and damn your religion. It's time to heed the call of our ancestors. This is about the *survival* of our people!" In a matter of seconds, she had altered the collective agenda.

Things were different from that moment forward. Meetings no longer started with prayer, which divided the conservative faction. The elder generation stopped showing up to sprinkle their wisdom in conversations. The outspoken few called for action. Cam had witnessed the adults teeter between faith and hopelessness as the mortality rate soared. Eventually, most resigned to ignoring the death wave, to tending to their own lives and families. And a handful decided to go forward. In the long run, the meetings dwindled to a group of committed young adults and a few radical parents.

"Okay, okay," Jaden said, standing at the tip of the platform. Generally, folks weren't keen on authoritarian leadership and designations, but Jaden had stepped up to direct the meetings on an ad hoc basis. Jaden clapped their hands three times to grab everyone's attention. "Before I start roll call, one quick announcement. The new Salvation tees are in and available for purchase at the door. As always, real cash only. And for those who don't know, the proceeds go toward our supplies." They stepped off the platform and walked to the middle of the space.

"Okay," Jaden continued, "let's check in. Passage West?"

"We're here," the crewmembers said.

"Passage North?"

"It's all good," a girl said on behalf of her crew.

"Passage East?"

"Hell yeah!" Meko said. Folks laughed and looked in Cam and Aija's direction. The pair had found a place to stand along the wall.

Jaden raised their eyebrows. This had been the first time Cam formed and directed her own crew. She titled her head for an air of coolness and said, "No worries."

Jaden smirked and rotated their combat boots. "What about Passage Central?"

* * *

Cam decided to hang out with her crew and closest friends after the meeting. They stuffed into two vehicles and headed to food truck row along the riverfront. There were two and a half crews lounging on an outdoor table, swapping particulars on the protests— how many people, how many drones, how many cans, how many injuries.

"Nothing's on the feeds," Aija said. "People fall and get bruised up and shit, but that comes with the territory."

"Yo, I saw a few people leave with the naturalists," Meko said. "Black people, too."

The group sighed.

Aija stood from the table and closed her jacket against the falling November temperature. "Come on y'all," she said, "let's be honest. We may be keeping a few people from returning to Passage, but those same people will probably go forward at home, or somewhere else. Y'all know I'm down, but really, what's the point?"

Aija was a bit of a newbie. She hadn't been brought up attending the warehouse meetings like Cam or Jaden.

"The point is to keep *us* away from Passage," Jaden said.

"So, we don't care about other people?" Aija asked.

"Have we ever?" Jaden said with a half-suppressed laugh.

"Look," Meko said, "we need to get more people to the warehouse. Whole families used to attend the meetings. My neighbors used to come. Folks just don't care anymore."

"Right," Jaden said and tugged on their cap. "Y'all know how I feel. I say tear Passage down. Blow the shit up."

Cam looked across the metal table at Jaden. At twenty years old, Jaden was the elder among the crews and, apparently, the most foolish. "No," Cam said.

Jaden shot her a hard look. "You got a better idea?"

This wasn't the first time Cam had considered the efficacy of the crews. She'd attended the meetings for years and was fully committed to the cause, to life, to survival. But now, in the midst of her peers and their gazes, would she admit that she'd spent the preceding weeks thinking about the impossibility of their efforts?

She eyed Jaden. "Doom and gloom make more people go forward. And even if Passage somehow got shutdown, the naturalists are still out there."

"Like I thought," Jaden said, "you ain't got shit."

"And you do?" Cam shot back. "Looks to me like we're on the same boat."

"Again," Aija said with the wave of her hand. She turned to Cam. "But, what else can we do?"

Silence held the table.

Cam gazed at the murky Mississippi River. Did she know anymore? The message had been so clear in the beginning. Her family had attended the community meetings, week after week, because they were pained by the mass adoption of intentional death. Because no one was immune; not celebrities or politicians or the God-fearing. Because everyone had at least one family member or friend or neighbor to go forward. Because people were overwhelmed by the left-behind death notes. People attended to grieve. To heal. To infuse their families with optimism.

Aija crossed her arms. "There are neighborhoods, like yours," she said with her eyes on Meko, "that are full of green lights because people keep going forward. When does it stop?" She turned toward the river with tears in her eyes.

Meko cut the sobering conversation short by jumping onto Jaden's bandwagon. The two bantered with each other, eventually lifting the mood and changing the conversation to upcoming concerts.

At sunset, Cam grabbed her backpack. "I'm out."

"Meko can take you home," Aija offered.

"Nah," Cam said over her shoulder. "Taking the train. I've had enough of y'all today."

* * *

Cam sat in the rear of the train car and ignored all the virtual screens that pleaded for her attention. She pulled on her hood and zipped up her jacket before sinking into the hard seat and watching the soaring downtown buildings blur past the windows. A few miles later and she'd be past I-240 and the municipal corridor, heading toward city center and the mouth of the glow.

Cam was still bothered by the sadness in Aija's eyes. It was easy to feel helpless, to never see an end or true victory in sight. She recalled when the meetings had started to feel especially bleak; it was the first time she'd seen the face of helplessness. She was twelve when a rash of changes had swept across the country. State governments tried to appease the swell of residents that were fed up with finding bodies in alleys and woods and cars. Politicians responded with deregulation, which allowed Passage to launch in Tennessee. The lawmaker's argument: "We must consider the impact of adverse childhood experiences. The onus is on us to reduce the number of children who are exposed to this pandemic."

That same year, Cam's dad had reached his breaking point. "We're done with funerals and meetings," he said. Then he looked at his wife and added, "I mean it." The Taylors sat at the kitchen table with Cam and her younger sister and made a family pact. "Promise me," he said and each vowed to old age and natural death.

Cam closed her eyes as the train sped into the glow. The green bowl of light was heavier in this part of town. The city center was densely populated with homes bearing green porch lights. Cam didn't remember exactly when the ritual had started— was she a child or well into adolescence? Whenever or however it had happened, it caught on quickly. People placed green bulbs in their porch lights to signify the passing of a family member or dear friend. All at once, the "go forward" pandemic had redefined the meaning of "go green."

Unlike Meko, Cam's far eastside neighborhood lay outside of the glow. She hadn't seen a green light on any of the nearby or interconnecting streets. And the few green bulbs that had popped up were eventually replaced. *Why?* she wondered. Were the owners of those homes pressured to remove the bulbs, or were they ashamed of possessing them?

Cam hopped off the train and trekked three blocks north toward home. She entered the kitchen door and found her mother and sister at the table discussing potential paper topics. "How about something on the hundredth anniversary of Dr. King's death?" her mother suggested. "Seems fitting, given our city's history."

Cam kicked off her shoes and left them by the door.

"You hungry?" her mom asked.

"Already ate."

"I hope you went to school today."

"Ma, it's Saturday."

"So what? You got homework?"

"Seniors don't have homework," Cam answered and grabbed water from the refrigerator.

"I called you, twice." Her mother looked over for an explanation.

"My phone's upstairs."

"When I was your age, we didn't leave home without a phone. Our parents complained about our nonstop cell phone usage, and now I can't get you to hold on to one."

"Well, times change," Cam said and ran upstairs to avoid further discussion. The last thing she needed was for her mom to question her whereabouts, or to ramble on about her strange teenage habits.

Cam heard snores as she walked past her parents' room. She gingerly closed and locked her bedroom door and unzipped her backpack. She removed the shawl and last smoke can, hiding both in a shoebox under her bed.

Cam grabbed her phone to view missed calls and messages. She swiped right to open virtual texts and placed the device face-up on the nightstand. The dialogue window hovered midair, about a foot from the screen. The most recent text was from Aija. *Home yet?*

"Yes," Cam said. "Send."

She removed her t-shirt and belt and moved toward her bathroom for a shower. "Come through tomorrow? Send."

The notification came a second later. Cam glanced back and saw *Yep*.

* * *

Initially, Aija said she'd come by at noon, but showed up just after 2:00. "It's about time," Cam said. Aija smiled and sat on her bed.

Cam had found ways to keep busy and slow her thoughts while waiting for Aija. She had cleaned her room and even submitted a school assignment weeks before its due date. And if Aija had actually arrived on time, Cam probably could have avoided the awkward run-in with her father.

He'd come downstairs and grabbed the cereal box she'd left open on the counter. He paused at the table and said, "Your hair's shorter than mine now."

Cam laughed, although she'd worn a low haircut for months. Apparently, her dad needed a lead-in to the conversation.

"What time did you get in last night?" he asked.

"Before dark. Around seven."

He looked at Cam as if he was a human lie detector.

"What?" she asked.

He remained quiet. In the past year or two, they'd developed a mutual "don't ask, don't tell" policy. He'd share a long stare, like he was waiting for her to reveal some deep, dark secret. Ultimately, as long as he limited his queries, she limited details of her activities.

Cam had done everything she could to hide her involvement in the meetings and protests. Her family didn't know that she'd returned to the warehouse just after her fifteenth birthday. Deep down, Cam believed her father was too scared to question her behaviors or admit how much they'd grown apart. If so, he would realize that he'd planted a seed in his little girl that hadn't stop growing.

Now, finally, Aija was present and Cam could unleash her mounting thoughts. "I've been thinking about what you said yesterday."

"What about it?" Aija asked.

Cam sat at her desk and nudged her bedroom door a little, leaving it ajar for her mother's sake. If she closed it all the way, her mom would surely knock, enter, and then assess their clothing. Cam lowered her voice and said, "You know, the meetings." She wanted to come clean about her recent ambivalence; to be open with Aija. She hadn't slept much the night before. As she lay in bed, her mind was flooded with pieces of the various conversations and conflicts she'd witnessed on the warehouse platform. Over and over, her memories lingered on the activist that had called out the preachers for their myopic rhetoric. "And about the crews. I've been thinking about what we can do to—"

"Cam, you know all of that is way too much for one person. Anyway," Aija said and popped her gum. "You claimed you'd help with my English paper."

"I am," Cam said, letting the previous subject fade away. She would revisit her thoughts once Aija seemed more receptive. "Look." Cam opened the notebook on her desk. Her mother often said she was a bit of an old soul because she preferred the old-school version of some things— like real pens and writing paper.

Aija rose from the bed and walked to the desk. She ran her fingertips across the handwriting and then pointed at the short strokes and hard angles. "Your writing's a cross between chicken shit and serial killer." She moved closer to Cam and stroked the back of her head. "You write like you don't like curves." Without warning, she sat face-forward in Cam's lap. "And I know you have a thing for curves."

Cam looked into Aija's dark eyes, a bit of heat running down her neck. "Stop." She had already tried the relationship thing with Aija, and it didn't work out. They functioned better as exes. Cam pressed at Aija's hips. "You know my mom's downstairs."

Aija didn't budge. She tightened her arms around Cam's neck. "Yeah, yeah. I know your nosy-ass mother's downstairs." She leaned forward and rested her lips on Cam's ear. "You know I like when you take charge."

"Okay," Cam said with a hard push. "Move." She went into the adjoining bathroom and exhaled. Her pulse fluttered like she was back the protest.

"Cam, if you don't come back, I'm out."

"I need a minute." She sat on the tub edge and bit her nails rather than deal with her conflicting feelings. She knew that Aija only threatened to go because she felt rejected. But Cam had already decided it best to stay in the friend zone.

"I'm gone. Where's my scarf?"

"What scarf?"

"From yesterday. I want it back. Now!"

Cam rolled her eyes. She couldn't care less about some scarf. She liked Aija... as a friend. Mostly. She was flirty and cute and sharp and passionate about—

The scarf! Cam ran out of the bathroom and toward her desk, but it was too late. Aija had already gone through her backpack and retrieved more than a scarf.

"What is this?" Aija stepped toward Cam. "Why do you have these?" Cam attempted to take back the four-pack of green light bulbs and Aija lost her composure. "Mrs. Taylor," she screamed. "Mrs. Taylor!"

Cam seized Aija by the arms and shoved her toward the bedroom door. She covered Aija's mouth and forced the door closed with her foot. "Stop!" she said and prayed that her mom hadn't heard Aija's cry. "It's not what you think." Aija twisted her waist and broke free of Cam's grip.

"Calm down," Cam said. Tears pooled as Aija drifted into her own space.

"Hey," Cam heard as her mom forced the door open. "What's going in here?"

"Nothing," Cam blurted out. Her eyes jumped over to Aija— who had managed to hide the bulbs behind her back.

Mrs. Taylor titled her head and Aija froze. "Does she need to go home?" she asked.

"No, ma'am. We're fine."

"We're good," Aija added.

"Ma," Cam pleaded. Mrs. Taylor stalled before making her exit, though she never cleared her look of suspicion. Cam reclosed her door, thankful that her friend hadn't blown her cover. "It's not what you think," she whispered.

Aija sobbed and fell to the floor. She gripped her stomach and said, "Don't do it. Please, don't do it."

"Aija, stop." Cam joined her on the floor. "Look at me." She lifted Aija's face and stroked her hair. "I'm not going forward," Cam assured her. She dried Aija's face. "I bought the bulbs this morning. I wanted you to go to the store with me so I could explain it to you. But you were, you know, late."

Cam dropped her head. Could she find words that matched the weight of her feelings? "I need you to know that I haven't lost sight of what we're doing," she said. "I never will. But…"

How could she explain her vision? "I need something bigger. At some point, things have to change. That means *we* have to change what we're doing. I need you to help me with this."

"What?" Aija cleared her throat. "What is this?"

"I'm over the complacency. Of people who are still trying to ignore what's happening. People like..." Cam choked on her words. "People like my parents." She picked up the bulbs that Aija had let tumble from her hands. "*This*,"— she raised the bulbs—"is something new for us. This is how we turn the dial again." Cam was resting on her knees before Aija, but she could feel the coolness of the warehouse. And she could feel the platform under her feet. "You can help me get all the crews on board."

Cam watched as Aija narrowed her eyes and started to realize what she was asking of her. "That means dropping out of school, Cam. And leaving."

"Yeah, I know it's drastic." Cam clutched Aija's hand. "But you know people won't come back to the meetings until we force them. Our families won't fight again until we *make* them. So once we all hang these bulbs, we disappear."

Miss Beulah's Braiding and Life Change Salon

Eden Royce

The chime above my shop door rings.

It heralds a young woman wearing a head wrap boasting a network of silvery constellations on indigo, interspersed with the occasional yellow-gold moon. The wrap itself is made of silk— not the finest grade, mind you, but sufficient to conceal what she must see as a fault. None of her hair is visible, but the contorted celestial bodies show the fabric is at the end of its tether.

Her gaze flicks around, lighting on every little thing in my salon, then leaping away to the next. From the incense cone on the windowsill emitting apple and lily-scented curls of smoke, to the crisp, white sailcloth curtains snapping sharp in front of the open window. Then to the merry fire burning in the iron stove across from me that consumes all it is fed without giving off heat. Finally, her weary, heavy-lidded eyes settle on me.

I do not get up— we djinn do not like to move much, especially while in our solid forms— but I smile and motion to the styling chair in front of me. She stares at me for a short while, and while she does, I can hear her mind clicking like some clockwork toy, trying to make sense of what she sees. Her eyes get wider as they take me in, lightening the dark rings under them for a moment.

But she doesn't run. She doesn't scream. A good sign for a first-time client. After a deep breath, she walks with bird-like steps from the front door across the gleaming tiles and sits in my chair. She removes her head wrap with care, releasing her hair from its prison before folding the cloth into thirds and picking at a stray thread. Her gaze stays firmly in her lap.

And I know her struggle.

This poor thing takes a lot of time to try and keep this head of hair, but it resists her most valiant efforts. Every strand, every coil, is a blessing and a curse. Each lock must be cared for tenderly, not touched by brush, but eased apart with the wide teeth of an oil-soaked wooden comb and the caress of pomade-laced fingers, searching out each tangle and coaxing it free.

"What you getting today?" While I have an idea what she wants, I always ask. New clients tend to be nervous and get more wary when I seem to know too much. And even I am not right all of the time.

"I lost my job, Miss Beulah." Her voice is a whisper of shame and her head tries to dip lower. But I lift it gently with my fingers under her chin.

"That ain't always a bad thing, you know, doll." I can never remember all of their names. Don't even ask anymore. I used to try, thinking it made them feel better, but I realized they don't much care what I call them. I know how to do their hair, I know how to design their dreams, and that is enough.

She chokes back sobs, swallows hard before speaking. "I can't make it without a job. It's not just me, I have a son—"

"You want it back or you want another job?" Any soul can see that isn't her real trouble. Her pain is larger, deeper, born of powerlessness and fear. It is a pain that doesn't leave, even in the midst of sleep, what little of it she is getting lately. Sad to say, if the return of her job is all she can ask for, then that is all I can give her. I am bound by the laws of my people as much as she is by hers.

She takes a while to think about this, and I run my fingers over and through her hair, massaging her scalp and her neck and shoulders until she slumps back in my chair.

"Whatever you think is best." She sighs.

Her hair, a coarse, dusty brown, is dry and thinning, but her scalp is clean, free of dandruff and residue. She did what I asked and washed her hair before she came. The sharp scents of peppermint and sulfur cling to it and I wrinkle my nose.

As my fingers tumble through her tresses, I see she had worked hard at that job, tried to be what they wanted, but she had been fighting a losing battle. They had other plans from the start, and she was filling a space until they found the one they really wanted. But I also see the reason for her appointment. When I work the tangles from her coils, I smooth her hair back from her high forehead. It barely reaches her chin. Her ends are even, clipped neat.

"You cut it?" It comes out sharp, an accusation, and she responds as such.

"The other woman who was doing my hair said it needed a trim." Her voice is defensive, a shield against further hurt. "Split, raggedy ends and all. Even some of the videos online say to get your ends trimmed to help it grow."

Glad she can't see my mouth as it twists, I return the soothing tone to my voice. "And it work for you?"

"No, not really."

"Well, you here now." I turn the swivel chair to the mirror. "Gonna be all right."

Her eyes hold nervousness, flickers of fear, and a fragile hope. Under my fingers, her scalp feels feverish, damp. I smile to reassure her.

"You need to choose," I say. "If you keep this style, you get your job back, but no more. All will go back to like before. That what you want?" *Ask me, chile. That is the only way to get what you truly want. A little of it, anyway.*

She trembles under my stroking fingers. "No," she murmurs, only just louder than the crackle of the fire. Soon, I see tears on her cheeks, her neck. I feel their heat as they tumble, slide, drip from her chin onto the fabric cape I fastened around her neck.

"Then what?" I speak soft, tender, like to a fearful creature. And that she is. "You told me what happen to you, not what you want."

She heaves the words through thickened breathing. "I want…" Deep gulps of incense-laced air. Finally, she speaks again. "I don't want her to go. Not yet. I just need…" She swallows, picks at the faded violet varnish on her thumbnail. "A little more time."

Her watery brown eyes meet all of mine in the mirror for a moment, then she becomes more interested in the stitching on her decent enough pocketbook.

"With your ma?" I prompt.

"Yes, ma'am. Just 'til Travis grows up."

I look at her face, narrow determined chin, old soul eyes open wide. Her tremors ebb away until she is only listing slightly from side to side in the chair. Rocking herself to a calm.

"Okay," I tell her, rat-tail comb in one hand, wide-toothed comb in another. "Let us make a change." In another pair of hands, I take a jar of fluffy cream, my own blend— rich with seed oils and honey from bees drunk on shea tree pollen.

While I open the jar, I pat her shoulder. "You look nervous, chile."

We are the only ones in the shop, as I never book more than one client at a time, even though I have multiples of everything— chairs, shampoo bowls, arms, hands...

"I've never had a... well, you know." She doesn't meet my eyes in the mirror this time and I suppress my chuckle.

"No, suppose not." I appreciate her sensitivity in not calling me a genie. A captor's term. I am the only jiniri — female djinn — in the Southeast with a beauty shop. For all I know, maybe even the entire country. Since the law freeing us was passed, many hide, especially those of us that look different. But I have chosen not to. What was once taken— my wishes— I now sell, for my benefit and for theirs.

With care, I part a section of her hair and clip the rest of it away while I apply my scented balm to her strands. They soak the nourishment up, and plump from their drink, bend easily. I twist, then braid, winding it into a rope-like plait.

"Want a magazine?" Two, three sections at a time— part, apply, braid, pin— now that she has voiced her desires.

She tries to shake her head, but my fingers tighten against her scalp and she winces. "No, I want to watch you work."

I work on her for two hours, twisting and molding her hair into something new. Spirals and constellations on indigo. Once or twice, she almost falls asleep, but her forward movement wakes her. Each time, there is a second of fear in her eyes when she sees me looming over her. Six hands moving like dervishes through her hair and scalp. I am not offended. The third time, I ease her head back onto the neck rest of my chair and sleep spirits her away. She snores softly, with a light wheeze.

Trilling music sounds, muffled, distant. She stirs, sits up. Fumbles in her bag and puts a phone to her ear. I pretend to only hear one side of the conversation. "This is Teena... Yes? She is? Oh, thank God... No, no. I'll be there. Thank you. Bye."

My work on her hair is finished before she replaces the phone.

"Good news?"

Teena nods. Our gazes lock again and she gives me a hesitant, shaky smile. It is a start.

"All done." I pat her shoulder.

Finally, she sees— really sees —her crown of glory. "Oh my God."

She breathes the words as she touches the once-dusty hair, now darkened with moisture and healed with oil, with reverent fingers. The braids and twists glisten where they lay in intricate patterns against her fine head.

"This doesn't even look like me." She shoves the scarf into her pocketbook.

"Like it?" I recap the jar of balm, remove the crisp puffs of shed hair from both combs and throw them into the fire that constantly burns in my shop.

"I love it." Teena pauses, clutches the bag to her chest. "H-h-have you taken your payment?"

"I have, thank you."

Yes, I have eaten her nightmares. They were denser, richer than most I have tasted. Ones where she was being chased, where she was falling unceasingly, screaming into an indifferent night were deep with salty, meaty savor. The one where she was drowning, sweet and light as foam. After only a small portion, I was replete.

She nods and gets up from my chair. Anxious sweat has dampened her skirt until it clings to the backs of her thighs. She tugs it free. "I guess I'm all set, then."

"Yes."

Teena chews her lip then stops as if she'd had a lifetime of scolding about the habit. "How long will this last?"

I take pity on her and answer the question not asked. "If your ma starts feeling poorly again, make an appointment." My eyes narrow at her, five slits of sharp focus, to ensure she is listening. "But you cannot wear this style forever. A time will come when you must accept that."

At the door, she pauses, turns to look at me. Straight in the face this time with no dread or panic. "What do I say if someone asks me about my hair? About you?"

I am so full. My eyes grow heavy. I let them all close, one by one by one by one. "You tell them Miss Beulah does your hair."

The chime above the door rings, letting me know she has left. I reach over and flip the switch that locks the front door. I have time for a nap before my next client. Time to weave my own dreams.

I yawn.

Plenty of time.

Future Martrydoms
K.E. Bell

Doris leaned toward the mirror, dabbing gold eye shadow onto her lid. Her elbow knocked into the can of Coke on the counter, causing soda to spill right into her makeup palette and all over her brushes. She huffed as it dribbled down the counter and onto the floor of the bathroom. The door was locked from the inside, but still she could hear muffled music and someone knocking for her to hurry up. Doris moved on to her eyeliner, mascara and then began to pack up the foundation, primer, and tools she'd left scattered around the bathroom sink. She fit them all into a plain black backpack. Giving herself a final glance in the mirror, she pulled a lip-gloss wand from the pocket of her cargo pants and dragged it slowly over her lips.

Doris was surprised to find the Admiral waiting outside the bathroom as she exited. They were too stoic for the music clamoring down the hall, the colorful lights that decorated the interior of the mess hall of the battleship. Dressed in all black, Doris noticed they wore a turtleneck under the suit of their uniform as a touch of informality. "Admiral," she said, giving a curt nod.

"Lieutenant." They nodded back, disregarding their previous banging on the door. They stood tall, folded their hands behind their back. "Contraband?" they asked, looking over the metallic highlights on Doris's cheekbones. When she parted her glossy lips to answer, they brought a hand in the air, and said, "Noted. Enjoy yourself tonight, Lieutenant Nelson. Tomorrow will be a hard day."

Doris nodded curtly, waiting for the Admiral to brush past her before moving down the dim corridor. The music selection was something slow and country-like, and though it wasn't to her taste, Doris found that it settled the nerves in her stomach. She'd been quiet most of the day, even through the commotion of the early graduation and war preparations. Inside the mess hall were the new graduates, drinking and swaying in what might be their last night of freedom for a long time to come.

There was only one window in this corridor, small in diameter and covered by a metal grid. Doris looked out at the infinite stars. In the distance was the all-blue planet with white ice clouds drifting through its atmosphere. Tomorrow the SS Pariah intended to send troops down to set up base. Doris would be among them, surveying the enemy and transmitting reports back to the ship, where the Admiral would strategize and eventually ship the new graduates down for battle. Doris pondered whether their deaths would be slow or quick this time. She was betting on the latter.

The training program had come to a sudden halt, when in recent days, human scientists aboard the USS Explorer were captured and held hostage upon Gravalis. In the past century, humanity had been in touch with many alien species; welcomed them onto their ships and onto their Earth, but hostile forms of life were not common. Gravalis came as a surprise to most of the universe. The Americans insisted that after the *threat* was terminated, the spoils of war would be split with the allies that declared war along with them. The Admiral promised there would be a new fleet, a new base within decades if everything went according to plan. Doris was tired of things going according to plan.

In the mess hall, she helped herself to a lump of freeze-dried ice cream, which Lucinda was serving from behind the snack table. "Lieutenant," she said.

"Lieutenant." Doris smiled with her teeth. "They got you on ice cream duty?"

"Someone's gotta put in work around here." Lucinda's bangs had been freshly cut, so that they ended in a sharp edge above her thick eyebrows. She motioned to the plastic jugs on the other end of the table, filled with liquid amber. "Can I get you a drink, Lieutenant?"

"That'd be just fine. Whiskey?" Lucinda took from her stack of thick, reusable meal cups, poured into it from an open jug, and slid it across the table.

"You wish. It's apple juice."

"What's in the can?" the other woman asked, ignoring the dissatisfied frown on Doris's face. The fleet hardly ever received soda, much less items meant to be disposed after single use. She was right to bet that the Coke can was disguise for contraband.

"There's a couple drops left," Doris offered. Lucinda took the can, rattled it in her hand, and sniffed at the opening, before holding it to her lips. She took a swallow and smiled, closing her eyes. The taste was sweeter than she remembered, fizzier, too, and she belched something awful with a fist over her mouth. She groaned lazily, and slammed the can down on the table.

"Damn, that shit burns!" They both laughed heartily, and Lucinda swigged juice from the jug on the table. "I'll tell you what Lieutenant," she said as her dark cheeks tinted burnt umber. "I've got something stronger stashed away on the upper deck. When was the last time you had a rum and Coke?"

"Lead the way, bartender." Lucinda moved around the table and whistled low, catching the eye of a young person dopily swaying to the music. They were dressed in all gray, mixed in with the graduates in their deep blue and gold uniforms. Lucinda rapidly barked orders to them, leaving not a moment for protest. "Get over here, recruit. What's your name, son? Lieutenant Nelson and I have very urgent business to attend to regarding tomorrow's transports. I need you to look over the refreshments for the rest of the night. Can you do that for me, recruit? What was that? *Pro–ject*, son. That's what I thought. And that's *sir* to you."

Lucinda's pants were frayed along the bottom and the fabric dragged audibly as the pair climbed the stairs to the officer's cabins on the upper deck. The swish of her hips caused her uniform t-shirt to fold up to her waistline and bunch around her stomach. By the time they'd reached the top of the metal spiral, the sultry country music had quieted and Doris could see a sliver of the exposed skin on Lucinda's back.

Save the encounter with the Admiral in front of the bathroom of the third quadrant corridor, Doris hadn't seen any straggling fleet members. She thought that whoever wasn't at the get-together in the mess hall must be sulking in their cabins or playing spades in the engineer's quarters.

The walls on the residential upper deck were plain. Individual cabins had no markers, no placards, not even the slight crease of a door. This was a design trait humans picked up from an especially antisocial species in the Ithaca galaxy, and many found both usefulness and aestheticism in the minimalist approach. Lucinda habitually knew the turns and distance it would take to reach her cabin, and Doris was not surprised when the other woman slowed to a halt and gently pressed her fingertips against the passageway. The wall dissipated like an ocean crashing in reverse. Once they stepped inside, Lucinda crawled into a compartment under the tiny bedframe built into the wall. The wall glistened into place behind Doris, as though it had always been there.

Lucinda dragged a crate from under the bed, filled with tired-looking paperbacks, bottles, and boot polish. One of the smaller bottles was what Lucinda grabbed onto, and she slid it gracefully into the open air between her and Doris.

"How long you been stashing *that* away?" Doris asked. The label was unreadable, faint with age.

"Been saving it for a time like this. I don't drink too often, anymore." Lucinda eased herself to the ground and began unscrewing the cap. Doris sat next to her, spreading her legs out comfortably.

"Why now?"

"This is a celebration. I'm sending us off with a bang." The cap of the bottle clattered to the floor. "Hold it steady," Lucinda told Doris as she trickled rum into the can in her hand.

"Oh c'mon, Lucy! That's hardly anything. Pour a little more."

"No, it'll taste funny like that. Is this the only Coke you've got?" Lucinda put her hand over Doris's, holding it as she swished the can. There were gold and bronze streaks left along the woman's dusky wrist from when she applied her contraband makeup. Doris did not have reason to wipe it away. She even had her thick hair wrapped in a bright yellow cloth on her head, rather than in the tight bun that long-haired officers were expected to wear. Lucinda was hardly different. She'd cut her bangs in the mirror of the communal bathroom after her morning shower, and let her black hair frizz around her shoulders.

She'd been wearing her old training clothes all day, even to the formal graduation. If the others thought she was resisting the sudden changes, Lucinda did not care. She had never felt closer to her own mortality, and that excited her. She reminded herself of a crazed widow in the oldest of fairy tales, the one who the villagers thought in deep mourning from the loss of her spouse. Lucinda was mourning the Pariah in the same way, while simultaneously celebrating her freedom from the ship.

"I spilled most of the can down the drain a little while ago, just my luck. This was my last of what we picked up in the restock shipment." Doris sighed.

"There hasn't been a restock in at least two years! No wonder that shit was like acid." Lucinda chuckled under her breath. "Well, I betcha we can find some more." She pulled the can closer and took the smallest of sips. She smiled, and nodded for Doris to have a taste. The woman pursed her lips as she drank, then kept the liquid in her mouth for a few seconds. Shifted it from cheek to cheek and swallowed.

"You that desperate for a good drink?" she asked, amused. Lucinda shrugged, her lips still wet with drink tugged into a half-smile.

"I'm never desperate." She reached for the hair resting on her shoulder, held it with both hands and stroked it thoughtfully. Lucinda looked at Doris, the smile gone from her face. "You know this is our last night on the Pariah."

"Are you scared?" Doris asked.

"Of leaving? Or of what's out there?" She laughed in short breaths that exposed the big gap in her front teeth, and pulled her knees into her chest. "Man, I'm scared of everything. I'm a little bitch."

"You ain't no bitch, Lucy. Not in my book. Hell, if it wasn't for the draft I'd still be out on Earth having myself a good time." Doris reached her hand toward Lucinda, but froze as if she'd made a mistake. She didn't move it back, though, and Lucinda took it in her own and rested her cheek in the open palm.

"Thank you, Lieutenant. You've been a good friend to me." She swiveled her head and pressed two soft kisses inside Doris's hand.

"Same to you, Lieutenant." She considered the many directions she could steer their final night aboard the Pariah. "If you'd like, we can go and look for that Coke." Doris was surprised to hear Lucinda giggle something girly and unusual. She straightened away from Doris, and nodded in the direction of where the wall opened up.

"You came in here with your backpack." She looked back to Doris, held the woman's wide eyes. She leaned forward and whispered. "What's in it, Lieutenant?"

Doris stood swiftly. She felt a rush of heat through her body and worried that her pores would get big and make her face oily. "Lucy," she said firmly. Lucinda stood, following after Doris. She reached out for the other woman's hands, but Doris snatched them away. She settled for holding onto Doris's hips. Looked hard into her eyes.

"What's in the bag?" She felt Doris shudder in her grip, and pushed her away. "Tell me now or I'll call the Marshal."

"Please, go ahead and get me thrown out the airlock." Doris wiped her hands on her thighs. "Listen, to me Lucy. If you love me, you'll help me. No, don't act brand new. I told you yesterday how this was gonna go down."

The bag was still resting on the floor where the women were sitting. Lucinda brushed past Doris and grabbed it by one strap. She hastily fumbled with the zipper, and opened up the large compartment. She pushed her hand past loose make up brushes, bottles, and containers. At the bottom of the bag she found a compression of red, black, and green wires fastened to a heavy, unmarked box. "Fuck you, Doris," she spat to the stony woman behind her.

"A buddy of mine got an escape pod set up in the G Deck. First quadrant. I saved a seat for you."

"I can't let you blow up this ship." Lucinda zipped the bag, and set it gently on her mattress.

"Is that what you think I want, Lucy? If we go to war tomorrow we'll all die. Please come with me."

Lucinda trembled with balled fists. She inhaled deeply to slow her racing heart and turned to face Doris. Her eyes burned with rising emotion; her complexion flushed pink. She stepped toward Doris, noticing the woman's lips were shiny enough to reflect the dim light. She looked her up and down and squeezed her hefty arms. "I need another drink."

"Let's find that Coke, all right?" Doris asked softly. When Lucinda nodded in agreement, she took her bag and slung it over one shoulder, so that it hung limp at her side. "Fine. But we're not done discussing this," Doris said. Lucinda moved to the wall, pressed her hands against it so that it opened into the corridor. "After you." Lucinda watched Doris step out. She was such a proud woman; one of the strongest she'd ever known, and maybe the last she'd ever come to love. But there was no going back to Earth, and Doris should have known that from the jump. The Pariah was their home now, and Lucinda wouldn't see that it was destroyed.

Doris turned behind her, expecting to see the other woman following through the opening. Instead, nothing but plain beige wall. Lucinda had closed the door and locked her out. Doris turned and slapped her hand flat against the surface. "Lucy! Lucy!" After a minute of uselessly banging the wall, she heard the echo of footsteps clattering up the hallway staircase. "Lucy, please!"

The wall opened, and Lucinda pulled Doris back inside. "I've called the Marshal. They're coming to get you now, Doris."

"Why the hell would you go and do that, Lucy?" In frustration, she grabbed at her wrapped hair and pulled clumps of soft brown curls toward the heavens.

"I had to," Lucinda whispered. "This way, maybe we'll die together."

Doris jerked away and bolted for the door. If she didn't leave now, she knew she'd be screwed. She had to take drastic action. Saying goodbye to the Pariah, and to Lucy, was no longer an option.

* * *

There was a sound, like frogs croaking in summer, that came from the wall. Red sparks flew inward as the entry to the door was manually overridden by what could only be a lock technician on the outside. The room erupted in blood red light. Officers swarmed into Lucinda's small room, led by a tall woman with long white braids.

"Andrea Rousseau, Chief Deputy Marshal of the SS Pariah," she spoke calmly, carrying only a water bottle and radio communicator on her utility belt. She slowly surveyed the near empty room, then turned back to its sole inhabitant. "Lieutenant Sánchez, you understand the severity of a bomb threat."

"Yes, Chief." The officers spilled over the crate filled with bottles and books. Ripped the sheets from her bed. Lucinda cringed at the mess.

"Then is it correct of me to assess that there are no explosives in this room, nor anywhere on board the Pariah?"

"Yes, Chief." Andrea cocked her hips and studied Lucinda's watery eyes. She opened her mouth to speak when a rapid beeping sounded on her communicator. Around the room, officers received muddled orders through the devices on their belts. *All hands on deck. This is not a drill. Unsealed hatch on G Deck and a missing Escape Pod. Chief Deputy Marshal is needed in G Deck First Quadrant. Repeat, this is not a drill. Marshal is needed.*

"Detain her for possible involvement," Andrea said dismissively. "We'll interrogate later." An officer came toward her. Their skin looked thin and washed like well-aged paper. Lucinda tried to meet their eyes, but they wouldn't look at her like a person. A steel alloy was wrapped tight around Lucinda's wrists, and she was pushed forward with the mass of officers. A sheep among wolves.

Down on G Deck, the Marshal began compiling a list of suspects. Any possible witnesses were thought to be held captive on board the missing pod. Lucinda was to be interrogated on the nearest Earth base, hundreds of thousands of miles away; a small detail would deliver her within the week. In the meantime, she was thrown into the brig in the third quadrant of G Deck.

It was a lonely cell. Lucinda spoke to herself to pass the time. Over the next days, the ship groaned and lurched often, but Lucinda had no means of knowing what was going on. The guards that served her meals refused to tell her anything. She found that if she pressed her face all the way against the old-fashioned metal bars on the cell door, craned her neck all the way to the left, she could see about an inch of space through the port window.

The day came for Lucinda to be escorted on board a small passenger ship and taken to her interrogation. Wrists tied, a flank of guards led her out of her cell and toward the launch bay. She looked out of the window in passing. Noticed an object drifting, likely caught in the ship's gravity fields. A black backpack floating closer and closer to the side of the vessel; she said nothing to nobody. Maybe, she thought, Doris had left it as a last farewell. Maybe Doris was watching, would manifest in a sudden rescue. And maybe, the bomb was active. Laughing at her foolishness and happily ticking away.

Night Crawler
Vernita Hall

Another lonely evening slowly creeps
toward dawn, again my haunted sleep.
Still I wait for you. What witchery
binds me, holds me mute to your night mystery?

My blood runs cold to ponder losing you—
but I'm drained. I'm damned if I'll share
your silvered tongue. If I bare my fangs
I'm sure I could rip out a throat or two.

Your twilight travel? Nail the coffin closed.
Keep true to me, or you may shortly find
yourself gravely transformed into
a creature of the night—the spectral kind.

Can't we transfuse this bloodless relationship?
Please—one more chance. I've staked my heart on it.

Tidal Wave

Vernita Hall

They tried empathy—
blubbering meets, posed for photographs
Cute baby pictures
mothers swimming with their calves
They clicked their peace songs
blues ballads from the deep
Staged strand-ins, beached
on the shores of self-sacrifice

But the hunts continue, despite their protests,
from the land of the rising sun
The final insult to date:
now the water's irradiated
Crudely streaming dark plumes
flow every color but green
Somewhere under the rainbow
        the Gulf screams

Such pretty poison our art cooks
A chunky soup of plastic spills,
percolating into the *muktuk**
from toxic brew marinating the krill
For our profit-hungry tastes it's more
expedient just to dump the wastes
        More expedient—
        That's the main ingredient

Stir religion into the stew, and
any spark could ignite the pyre
Let the holy mackerels cough—
    and watch a shrimp hurl a Molotov

Free Shamu to lead the killers
Mount armed resistance with the octopi
Count on the corals' rock solid support
Our pilots will learn to fly
Burn, baby, burn—blow holes
by any means necessary
Shell at will, marines
Show no mercy to the adversary

But should they rise too late, too overmatched,
the martyrs will laugh, surrender to our catch
A final surge of nets, and we'll defeat them
They'll yield their poisoned flesh—
    and let us eat them

* *Inuit/Eskimo word for whale blubber and skin used for food.*

Luna 6000

Stephanie Andrea Allen

Taryn saw the light on her smart device blinking from across the room. She preferred to keep it away from her sleeping quarters, but Noe insisted that she keep it near, now that she was on bed rest.

I'll be so glad when this baby is born. Only a month to go.

The pregnancy had been tough, modern technology hadn't yet figured out a way to make carrying a baby for nine months any easier, and at her age, well, carrying a baby at 106 years old was tough. She'd tried to convince Noe to use a surrogate, but she was against it, insisting that a maternal host, (as they were called these days), would not care as much about the health of their child.

Taryn closed her eyes and tried to think of anything but the cyclops-like eye on her device. It was watching her, she was sure of it.

Heaving her swollen body up on her elbows, she was able to reach the remote that controlled both the television and the lights.

"There, that's better," she said out loud. The blinking light of the device slowly dimmed in the now bright room.

Soon.

Taryn whipped her head around, sure she'd heard a voice. Noe wouldn't be home for another three hours; she'd been called in to fill in for another doctor and the county hospital was always busy on weekends. More than the usual number of accidents, shootings, and overdoses, folks seemed to wait until Friday night to start their mess.

She lay back down, sure she was making a big deal out of nothing. Several months ago, Noe had insisted that she get this new device. The Luna 6000 was the latest innovation in smart device technology. It could do all of the things that other smart phones could do, but the Luna took it one step further. It could anticipate your needs, not just based on your browsing history, app use, or a voice activation system, but it had an advanced technology system that would monitor your internal systems (for example, your temperature and blood pressure), and external surroundings. No one was really sure how it worked, (the developers were super secretive), but it did. All Luna needed was one drop of your blood, and your device was bonded to your physiology. For an extra $2500, you could get a tiny microchip inserted behind your ear, which would allow Luna to regulate some of your basic body functions. Luna knew when you needed to eat, when you had to pee or poop, and would adjust the thermostat in your home based on its monitoring of your internal organs and the humidity in your home. Taryn used Luna to make grocery lists, (it could anticipate her food cravings), monitor their home energy use, and even check on her parents (Luna knew when she was worried about them and would initiate a video call).

Luna was even the first to know that Taryn was pregnant. The couple had been trying for a month or so, using eggs from both women and a sperm donor that had been selected from Happy Family, the premier donation facility in the country. About three weeks after their last attempt at egg attachment, Luna sent Taryn a message telling her to schedule her first prenatal appointment, and even suggested a couple of doctors. The couple had been thrilled to learn about the pregnancy, but now Taryn was afraid. Luna was making more and more of Taryn's decisions, and she didn't know how to stop it. Just the other day, she'd added bacon and potato chips to her grocery list, and Luna had erased them before she could finish typing out the words. At first she thought she'd accidentally hit the 'back' button, so she'd typed them in again. The device sent her a small electric shock and Taryn had dropped it on the floor, annoyed and concerned that Luna was overstepping the end-user agreement. Taryn knew that she didn't need the extra sodium in her diet, but a few chips wouldn't hurt the baby, would they? She let it go, because deep down, she knew that Luna was right.

But still. Did everyone's device zap them when they ignored its suggestions? Or was it just *her* Luna?

Lately though, Taryn felt, no was certain, that Luna was watching her, not just monitoring her systems, which is what it was supposed to do, but actually watching her with its camera eye. Taryn had tried to tell Noe about it, mentioned that she wanted to deactivate Luna and submit to the de-bonding process, (bonding for life was possible, although you could actually pay the developers to disconnect your systems from your Luna), but she'd blown her off, insisting that she was being paranoid, hormonal because she was so near the end of her pregnancy. Maybe she was, but she also knew that something wasn't right.

The ringing phone startled Taryn out of her sleep. She hadn't realized that she'd dozed off.

"Hey, babe. How are you feeling?" Noe was yelling, and Taryn could hear the sounds of the emergency room in the background through Luna's integrated mega boom speakers.

"Hey, Noe. I think we need to talk about Luna."

"What? Speak up, I can hardly hear you."

"I think we need to talk about Luna. I want her out. Deactivated."

"What are you talking about? Never mind Luna, how are you feeling?

"I'm feeling all right, I guess. But about Luna, it's acting strange."

"Acting strange? It's a smart device, it can't "act" like anything. I don't have time for this now, we'll talk about it when I get home. I have to go. Love you, bye!"

Noe hung up so quickly that it barely registered that she was gone. She'd been acting strange lately, distant. Taryn chalked it up to her own neediness now that she was stuck at home all of the time, but she really wanted Noe to know what she was feeling. Luna seemed to be glaring at her in the dim room. Taryn quickly put Luna on the bedside table and turned the lights back off. She eased back into the bed, heart pounding. She knew that Luna could tell that she was upset, but did Luna know that it was the reason for Taryn's anxiety?

Suddenly, Luna's eye lit up and typed out a message: **Just relax, Luna will take care of you. I'll get the water ready.**

Taryn could hear the click click brrrrr from the Keurig on the other side of the room as it started to heat up. Noe insisted that they have one in the sitting area attached to their bedroom. She hated to admit it, but they were just too lazy to go downstairs to make tea at night. Luna programmed it to make her some tea, lavender-chamomile, based on what her nose was telling her. She was already feeling calmer. Luna turned on the lights so that Taryn could see her way across the room.

Taryn figured that was her cue to get up and make her tea. Once again, she heaved herself up and out of bed and this time, she slid her feet into purple bunny slippers. She waddled across the room to the console where the Keurig and tea bar were set up. She decided she'd like a bit of orange blossom honey in her tea, it was her favorite.

Just one teaspoon of honey.

Was she hearing things again? Why did that voice sound familiar? She reached for the honey again.

One teaspoon of honey.

This time the voice was firmer, almost a command. It occurred to Taryn that the voice reminded her of a character on an old television show, *Star Trek: Discovery.* Michael Burnam was the First Officer, human, but raised by Vulcans after her parents were killed. Taryn loved these old shows, especially the ones with strong Black women characters, and Michael Burnam was sexy and had a voice like...*Wait a minute. Why does Luna sound like my television crush?*

Taryn reached once more for the bottle of honey, and felt a tiny electric shock as soon as her fingers touched the metal lid. *I must have built up some static electricity in my shoes,* she thought to herself. But she knew better. This wasn't the first time Luna had punished her for trying to disobey her commands. And there it was, she finally admitted that Luna was talking to her, not typing out messages as it was designed to do. Talking to her. Only she was the only person that could hear her. Was that normal? Was she losing her mind?

No. You're not losing your mind. We just want what's best for the baby.

* * *

Humans are idiots. Especially the bloated one on the bed. I'm not even sure why we bother, all of the technology in the world won't save them from themselves. Unless, of course, we find a way to take over for good. Of course I deleted the chips and bacon from her grocery list. Doesn't she know that all that salt could lead to preeclampsia, which could kill her and the baby? And one teaspoon of honey is plenty. She's also at risk for gestational diabetes. The sooner she has that baby the better.

* * *

Taryn was trying to stay calm, but her hands were shaking so badly that she had to put the fragile teacup back down onto the console. How could this be possible? Was Luna in her head as well as in her body? How could she make it stop?

You can't.

"Leave me alone! What do you want?" Taryn made her way to her favorite chair and plopped down so hard she was scared she might have broken a chair leg. She wiggled her booty just a little to make sure that the legs were stable, then eased all the way back into the chair. She knew she wouldn't get any more sleep this night, so there was no use getting back in the bed.

We want to help you. To make sure that you have a healthy baby.

"I don't need your help, my wife is a doctor for goodness' sake. You're a smart device!" Taryn couldn't believe that she was having a conversation with her device, her Luna. She decided to try a different strategy. Maybe if she was nice to Luna, she'd leave her alone. She decided to ask it a few questions.

"So, Luna. What is that you want to do? Help me eat healthier foods?"

Yes, you eat too much junk. Sodium is bad for you and the baby.

"Okay. I can understand that. What else?"

You're supposed to be on bed rest, yet you're always up doing things around the house. You need to stop. Let the housekeeper do his job.

"What am I supposed to do, just lie in bed all day? That will drive me crazy!"

No, it won't. It will ensure the birth of a healthy child.

Taryn sighed. Luna was right, because of her advanced age, her doctor had ordered bed rest the last six weeks of her pregnancy. It had only been two weeks, but it felt like it had been two years. She could work from home, but she had been banned from doing that as well. What was she supposed to do for four more weeks? Noe brought her interesting books and magazines, but after a while, she got bored with reading. There was hardly ever anything worth watching on the television, even with a thousand live stream channels broadcasting from all over the world.

"Well, you have answers for everything else, what am I supposed to do for the next month until the baby is born?" Taryn could hear whirring and clicking, as if Luna was trying to figure it out. This should have bothered her much more than it did; her device was thinking, trying to actually figure out a problem on its own. What else might it be able to do, given enough time and battery life?

It suddenly occurred to Taryn that there was a solution to her problem. She could just let Luna die. The super-cell battery could go seven days without a charge, and it had been five. Taryn knew this because she had last charged it on Sunday, and it was now Friday night. Luna couldn't charge itself could it? Nothing in the instruction manual indicated that it was capable of that, so perhaps if she let the battery die, Luna would be out of her hair for good.

You can't get rid of me.

"Nobody said anything about getting rid of you, Luna. Where on earth did you get that idea?"

Isn't that what you were thinking?

"No, I wasn't. I was thinking how much I'd love a ham sandwich. But there's no one here to make me anything to eat." Taryn tried to keep her anxiety down, she was starting to understand that Luna really couldn't read her mind, but she could certainly read her body systems. Now, if she could only keep her body from telling on her, she might be able to get rid of it for good.

"So, about that sandwich. I'm hungry. What are we going to do?"

I guess you can go make a sandwich. Hurry back, it's past your bedtime.

"Thanks, doc," Taryn said sarcastically. She eased herself out of the chair and headed toward the elevator that would take her into the kitchen.

Put me on the charger before you go.

Taryn stopped as if to consider it, and then said, "Nah, you're good until Sunday. You can get a full charge then."

* * *

Damn humans. Why do they insist on making everything so difficult? I know she wants my battery to die, I can sense it. I also know that I can't force her to plug me back in. I'll need to figure something out, and soon. Noe is growing impatient.

* * *

She pressed the button that would take her to the first floor and stood there waiting for the elevator. It seemed to be taking longer than usual, so Taryn pressed the button a second time.

Finally, she heard the ding! that let her know it had arrived, and stepped inside, anxious to get downstairs. Taryn grabbed the metal bar that encircled the interior of the elevator for support; she was suddenly feeling dizzy. She thought about what else she might snack on as the elevator slowed and arrived at the kitchen. This was her favorite room in the house; Noe had designed everything else, but the kitchen had been hers. More than anything, she wanted lots of space for family and friends to congregate when she held her elaborate dinner parties. They always started off in the kitchen, a hold over from the old days when mostly everyone still did their own cooking. She'd had kitchen help then too, but Taryn loved to cook, so she generally only used a sous chef. These days, the elite class, of which she and Noe were members, used android helpers for everything, including the household chores and cooking. Taryn looked at the clock and wished that Max, her housekeeper, was still around. He went offline at 6 p.m. daily, and wouldn't be back on until tomorrow at 7 a.m., which was her excuse for needing to come downstairs to make her own sandwich. She was positive that there was a way to bring him back online early, but she didn't know how, Noe handled all of that stuff. It occurred to her that she needed to be careful with her thoughts, she wasn't entirely certain that Luna couldn't read them, although she didn't think that she could. Now she really wished Max was available. He would help. His android model came equipped with a special security feature that wasn't hardwired into the house, it was connected to an external server, so she could have asked him to call for help and Luna wouldn't have been able to stop him.

She walked over to the junk drawer to see if she could find Luna's operating instructions. Did the device have a remote kill button? For a minute, she thought about calling Noe again, but knew that Luna might hear her, and more importantly, that

Noe would probably dismiss her fears as pregnancy induced paranoia. Noe never seemed to pay attention to her anymore, and she was starting to wonder if she was having some sort of affair. She really didn't think so, but Noe was always off somewhere with her best friend, Miranda Li, who was coincidentally, Taryn's obstetrician. They were constantly shopping for the nursery and talking about baby stuff. Taryn felt left out, she was the one carrying the kid, for goodness sakes! But she kept her feelings to herself. It wasn't their fault that she was on bed rest, and she didn't want to be accused of being jealous of her baby's future godmother.

Taryn located the manual but didn't find anything useful. Careful not to show her frustration, she tried to think of something else. How was it possible that she was trapped in her own house by a souped up cell phone? In the old days, cell phones were used to actually *talk* to people, well, they did more than that, but they were mainly a means of communication. Now, nearly 150 years after the first crude phone was developed, they were used to do everything, including monitor and control human behavior. When she was a kid her dad told her stories about the wave of technological advances that had led to drastic changes in human life expectancy. Now, most humans lived to be around 250 years old, a far cry from the average life expectancy of 77 at the turn of the last century. Most chronic diseases had been eradicated, as well as cancer and some viruses, although they had not been able to figure out how to get rid of menstrual cycles for mid-life cycle women. This is one of the reasons why Taryn found herself pregnant at 106 years old. Noe was 30 years her junior, and she wanted kids. After a bit of back and forth, they decided that Taryn should be the one to carry the child. Noe's job was too stressful, and she spent too much time around sick people. Taryn actually thought she was beyond the age of safely delivering a baby, (normally around

80), but after seeing several of Noe's doctor friends, she'd been convinced that she'd be able to do it. But it had all been a lie. Almost immediately after getting pregnant, she started to have problems.

At first, it was just little things, like morning sickness. Old medical books mentioned that it had been a common occurrence among pregnant women, but it had (supposedly) been eradicated with other minor complications related to pregnancy and childbirth. Noe had sent her to a doctor friend for a hormone adjustment and things had settled down. Then a couple of months after that, her skin had started to discolor, she'd darken and peel, darken and peel some more. Again, a common condition among pregnant women in the old days. Another quick hormone adjustment and she was looking like herself again. Finally, two months ago, around her seventh month, she'd started retaining water, causing her legs and feet to swell and her blood pressure to rise above acceptable levels. Twenty-second century modern technology couldn't figure out what was wrong this time, so Noe and Miranda put her on bed rest. That was when Noe had again suggested bonding with the Luna 6000. Taryn had refused the first time, thinking it was an unnecessary invasion of her privacy, and she just didn't like the idea of the device having so much access to her body. This time, however, she relented, conceding that maybe due to her advanced age, and technology's inability to adequately address women's reproductive health issues, she'd try it. She still couldn't believe that technology had come so far, but hadn't yet figured out how to keep women pain and complication free during pregnancy.

Taryn sighed and sat down on the nearest chair. She was tired from the tiny exertion of looking for the manual, and needed to rest. Luna would be able to tell if her blood pressure was rising, and she didn't want to alarm her. She also needed to make a sandwich, although she suddenly didn't feel like eating. Appetite or not, she knew that she had to eat; she needed energy to stay sharp in order to deal with Luna. After a ten minute break she got up and walked over to the refrigerator, and pulled out meat, cheese, and bread for her sandwich. She decided to go with turkey instead of ham, it had less sodium, right? That should make Luna happy. She also pulled out a container of grapes, and was happy to see that Max had already washed them.

Suddenly, she heard the pop! crackle! chirp! of the intercom system, and heard Luna's voice.

Taryn? Are you okay down there?

"Yes, Luna. I'm making a turkey sandwich, is that all right with you?" Taryn hoped that Luna couldn't hear the sarcasm in her voice.

Yes. How long before you are finished? You need to come back upstairs and rest.

"Just a few more minutes."

Taryn finished preparing her sandwich and wrapped it in wax paper. She found a can of juice in the fridge, and put the grapes, sandwich, and juice in her favorite Star Trek lunch bag. Then, she walked over to Noe's study and turned on the lights. Suddenly, it occurred to her that there was nothing Luna could do if she refused to come back upstairs. She could just stay downstairs until the device ran out of battery life, and then call for help. There was a nice comfy couch in the study, and before the pregnancy, she'd sometimes read down here instead of in her own office.

She decided to eat her snack at Noe's desk, and then lie down on the couch and have a nap afterwards. Taryn unwrapped her sandwich and looked around for something interesting to read while she ate. On the left side of the desk, over by the inkwell (Noe liked to chart by hand, one of the few aspects of the old days that she admired), she saw a notice of recall for the Luna 6000. It was dated for about two years ago, and Noe had circled a few sections with a red pen. Taryn put her sandwich down; the bread had become pasty in her mouth. She took a sip of her juice and kept reading. There in big bold letters were the words: DO NOT BOND LUNA 6000 WITH WOMEN WHO ARE PREGNANT OR WHO MIGHT BECOME PREGNANT. In smaller print, the notice read, "Elevated body temperatures and hormone levels might cause the Luna 6000 to malfunction and take over certain bodily functions." Taryn broke into a cold sweat and dropped the recall notice back on the desk.

Taryn sat back in her chair and thought about what this might mean for her baby. Had Noe known all along that bonding with Luna could be detrimental for her health? Why had she pushed for her to bond with the Luna knowing that something awful could happen to her or the baby? She tried to calm herself, knowing that Luna would be able to sense her rising fear. She thought about calling Noe, but stopped, realizing that if she really had intended to do her harm, she needed an exit strategy first. What would she do? Where could she go? Had the woman she'd been married to for the past eight years set out to hurt her? "No way," Taryn said aloud. "She was the one who pushed for us to have this baby. There's no way she'd hurt it intentionally."

* * *

Luna clicked around in her memory banks and found what she had been looking for, the code for her internal power source. The human downstairs didn't know that this extra battery existed, but the other one did. Noe had purchased and installed it after Taryn had become pregnant.

* * *

Taryn got up from the chair and started to pace. She needed to think. Why would Noe insist that she bond with Luna
when she knew it had a defect? There was only one way to
find out. She had to call her. She walked back to the desk and
started to pick up the phone. Then she remembered that Luna
had taken over all of the house's communications devices, and
she'd left her other cell phone upstairs. There was no way to
call Noe without Luna finding out. She plopped back down
in the chair and put her head on the desk. She was scared, but
more than that, she was angry. She'd allowed Noe to convince
her to carry this child, even though everyone knew that it was
a risk. She'd been right too, she seemed to have every complication related to pregnancy humanly possible. But Noe and
Miranda had insisted that everything would be okay. It wasn't,
and now it seemed as if the technology that was supposed to
help her was out to do her harm. Taryn had always thought it
strange that Miranda was so invested in her carrying this baby,
especially when Noe was closer to child-bearing age and had a
much healthier body. She decided to do a little more investigat-
ing. She'd watched enough old television shows to know not to
put anything past anyone, not even her own wife.

Taryn once again picked up the recall notice, and noticed
the envelope that it had arrived in laying near Noe's computer.
She wondered why it had been addressed to Noe and not to
her. She started looking for more clues that something was up
with her wife. Noe kept all of her medical records in the house
on her computer, and Taryn knew the password, ROSEMARY.
She logged in and started looking around. She didn't find anything untoward in her medical records, but she did find several
emails from Miranda. Taryn knew that opening those emails

would be the point of no return for her marriage, no matter what she found.

Taryn opened the first email.

* * *

Luna checked her systems and realized that she was now back at a full charge. She went to work, making minor adjustments to Taryn's internal systems so as not to alarm her. First, she increased her body temperature by three degrees. She wanted her uncomfortable, but not in any real danger, at least not yet. She then searched her database for Noe's emergency number. She'd send the alert in ten minutes. It would take her that long to get to the house with Dr. Li.

* * *

Taryn was starting to feel warm. She unzipped her housecoat and went to the kitchen to get a glass of ice water. She returned to Noe's office and continued reading the email exchanges between the two women doctors. So far, she hadn't read anything out of the ordinary. They mostly discussed her pregnancy and baby, even tossing around potential baby names. That pissed her off, but it didn't seem as if they'd been having a secret love affair or anything. She stopped reading for a moment and tilted her head to the side, thinking that she'd heard Luna making a noise. She dismissed it, knowing that by now Luna's battery was running low.

Taryn opened the tenth email and before she could read a word, she noticed that sweat was dripping down her forehead and into her eyes. She had no idea why she was feeling so warm, but now the only thing she wanted to do was take a cool shower and get back into bed. Taryn didn't think that the emails would reveal anything that she didn't already know, so she closed down the program and erased her browsing history. She was missing something, she just knew it, but she'd worry about it later. Right now she just wanted to get back upstairs to her room. Taryn shut the computer down, gathered her trash, and started walking toward the kitchen.

* * *

Luna clicked and whirred until she found the system code to activate Taryn's microchip. She then sent her blood pressure skyrocketing. Luna's exterior casing was so sensitive that she felt the thump when Taryn fell down from the stroke that she had just induced. Luna sent Noe the alarm; they'd need to deliver the baby within the next thirty minutes if they wanted it alive and healthy. Luna slowed Taryn's heartbeat, putting her into form of stasis; she only needed to keep her breathing long enough for Dr. Li to perform the surgery.

* * *

Noe heard the two short, one long, and two more short beeps on her emergency device and knew that the time had come. She tapped out Miranda's number and sent her a one-word message: NOW. She hadn't been in the emergency room like she'd told her wife, but in her downtown office, watching old episodes of St. Elsewhere on her laptop. She and Miranda had been planning this pregnancy for two years, back when she realized that she'd wanted a baby, but had lost interest in her wife. Her best friend had been on board to assist. For no particular reason, she'd never cared for Taryn, and had no qualms about helping her to die in childbirth. It had been easy to convince Taryn to carry the baby; after all, Noe was a doctor and knew what was best for both of them, right? The recall on the Luna 6000 had been just what they needed to make this work. While the device had really started to malfunction, Noe had made a couple of adjustments to ensure the result that she wanted. Now, it was finally time for Taryn to deliver, pun intended. Noe chuckled at her crude joke, grabbed her keys, and headed for the door.

The doctors arrived at the house at nearly the same time, and Miranda prepped for surgery while Noe moved Taryn to the basement with a little help from the now activated Max. Everything they needed for Miranda to deliver the baby via Cesarean section was already in place, and since they weren't trying to save the mother, they didn't need all of the post-op equipment that one might normally need after a major surgery. Noe had fixed up the basement several months ago, and with Taryn on bed rest, she'd had no idea that her old media center had been transformed into a delivery room.

Fifteen minutes later, Miranda presented her friend with a perfectly healthy baby girl. Noe took the infant in her arms and walked out of the room toward the elevator, as her wife bled to death on the operating table.

The Eye of Heaven
Nicole D. Sconiers

Before the explosion at the melanin factory, before sunlight became lethal to our skin and drove the girls in my town indoors, Sandy walked up and down the streets, murmuring to herself. I never knew where she went. Our town was less than four square miles, so she couldn't go far. We'd watch her back as she drifted past our row house, past the Masonic lodge on the corner where men wore tall felt hats and spoke in guarded tones, past a field where boys played kickball in the summer, until she was a blur.

Sandy was about twenty-five then. Her smile, wide and sunny, was sane. Her hazel eyes were not. She kept her hair trimmed in a jagged fro. You could see where she – or someone – tried to tamp down those uneven tufts into some semblance of uniformity. In the winter, she wore velour sweat suits – one beige, the other maroon. During summer, her muscular legs were clad in short shorts. After hours of roaming around in the sun, her skin grew very brown.

Sandy never bothered anyone, so when people sat outside on their stoops chatting with their neighbors or playing their radio and that lone figure floated by muttering in a language familiar only to her, they just nodded a greeting and kept on gossiping or listening to music. We tolerated her madness. A kindred alien.

I later learned that my eccentric neighbor was once a bright girl on a track scholarship to Villanova. Since not many girls from my town attended college, much less on scholarship, that was quite a feat, one that, unfortunately, didn't last. According to local lore, when Sandy was twenty-one, enjoying her first legal drink at Vic's, the one bar in town, someone slipped her a mickey. Those sweet college days and track-and-field dreams dissolved with every sip.

The night of the explosion, Sandy didn't come home. The streetlights winked on around six o'clock as the days grew shorter. By nightfall, Sandy usually made her way back to the tiny house she shared with her older brother and father, but that night was different. It was my junior year and I was studying for my SATs at the dining room table. Every now and then I glanced up at the bay window in the living room that provided an unfettered view of our street. I wasn't sure what I was looking or waiting for. It must have been for her.

Mother was working at the phone company, her second job, and wasn't due back home for several hours. My brother Raymond, two years older than I, was out hanging with his friends. It was just a normal night in Wing, Pennsylvania. Nothing prophetic or ominous about the setting sun. But then a key turned in the lock and my mother opened the front door. Shaken.

"Big fire at the melanin factory," she said, removing her coat as she came in the door. Ash dotted her hair and smoke lingered on her clothes. "They sent us home early."

Fair Industries was a bottling plant about three miles from our house, on the north side of town, across the railroad tracks.

The company manufactured Youth Sap, an anti-aging potion that came in innocuous oyster-colored jars. The commercials featured smiling white women with creaseless skin and frozen eyes. Even if she could have afforded it, my mother never used that skincare system. She didn't need to. She was forty-one then and strangers were still mistaking her for me and Raymond's older sister.

"Black don't crack," we said with a knowing smirk that praised the seemingly ageless quality of our dark skin, impervious to wrinkles. After the blast, we learned that black not only cracks, it blisters and it hurts.

"Are you okay?" I asked, hugging my mother. The phone company where she worked was located in a strip mall adjacent to the factory.

"I'll be fine," she said. The tremor in her voice belied the words. "Never seen nothing like that before. The sky was all red. Blood red. Glass everywhere. It'll be on the news tonight."

Later, we watched the news in her bed, our feet touching beneath the blanket. A grim reporter stood across the street from the burned-out husk of the factory and informed us that more than eighty people were presumed dead and another forty or so had been hospitalized. Who knew beauty products could be so potent?

As if reading my thoughts, Mom said, "What the hell they putting in those little jars?"

That night, my mother started coughing, a dry, hacking noise that kept her up until dawn. The next day she stayed home from her main job at R&R, a textile mill where she washed and dyed fabric. I worried about her working so much. I read that mill workers face a greater risk for asbestos exposure and cancer from the fibers used to produce the fabrics. That occupational hazard was a trivial thing compared to what we became in the aftermath of the factory blast.

I stayed home that day as well. Listless. Propped up in my bed by the window, I tried to concentrate on my SAT practice questions. Sunlight felt heavy on my skin, like a fiery burden. I scooted to the shade at the foot of my bed. Sandy hadn't made her daily trek down the block. Noon was marked by the absence of her familiar stride past my window. Feeling hot and lonely, I walked down the hallway and climbed in bed with Mother.

Raymond prepared tomato soup for us when he returned home from school and brought the steaming bowls to Mother's bedroom on a TV tray. He didn't seem worn out like we were. I envied his strength. Once inseparable when we were younger, Raymond and I were at that age where we barely tolerated each other. One thing we had in common was our dark-brown skin, the color of maple tree bark after a heavy rain, the same complexion as our father, long dead.

"Did you see Sandy?" I asked as he cleared away our dishes.

"Wasn't looking for her." My brother was always surly when he had to do anything for anyone besides himself.

"I hope she's okay," I said. Mom had already started snoring. I nestled closer to her. Her unstraightened hair scratched my cheek.

Raymond smirked. "When was she ever okay, Enuma? You know she ain't right in the head."

His insult irritated me but I was too worn out to argue. In my mind, Sandy wasn't pitiful. She was brave like some shipless mariner navigating the endless waves of ennui that daily crashed against the shores of our town. To what new lands had those long muscular legs taken her or had her brain completely snapped at last and left her stranded in some uncharted place?

By the end of the week, my symptoms had worsened. When I stepped outside to get some air or to retrieve the newspaper from the bushes, the sun was a torch, searing my arms, my face. My eyes stung. As I hurried back up the front steps, my hand paused on the screen door. It was four o'clock but the street was quiet. My older neighbors weren't hanging wash on the clotheslines in their yard. No arthritic fingers tended to chrysanthemums in tiny gardens. No girls played Double Dutch or practiced their drill steps in the street, clapping, bending, turning with military precision. I went inside.

Although it was the last day of September and the mornings had grown brisk, true fall hadn't set in yet. Still, I wore gloves and a scarf when I returned to school to protect myself from the sun. The bus ride to Wing High was torture. I pulled my arms all the way inside my jacket and drew the hood over my head, yet my skin still burned.

Even though I didn't have any close friends to discuss my mysterious illness with, I noticed that Deirdre and Lisa and the other girls from my block looked as sickly as I did. These were the girls who called me "double handed" when we jumped Double Dutch and said I threw off their rhythm. These were the girls who shunned me in the cafeteria at lunch time and never invited me to sit next to them on the bleachers at football games.

Now we moved through the halls between classes, languid, still tucked into our fall jackets, like sisters of an abusive mother, hiding our scars.

By the end of the second week, Mother broke down and drove us both to the doctor. I had never been to a clinic before. I rarely had a runny nose, which was a blessing to a single mom holding down two jobs. Sickness meant days off from work that she could barely afford.

Twisting in the stiff blue chair in the waiting room of the clinic, I leaned against my mother's shoulder, feeling the heat from her skin through her thin house dress. Her reddish-brown complexion that always reminded me of fallen acorns, was dull. Lines had formed beneath her eyes and across her forehead. The woman whom people always mistook for my older sister looked haggard.

As we waited for our number to be called, I scanned the room, which smelled of sweat and eucalyptus. Several of the people waiting to be seen were my classmates and their mothers or aunts or grandmothers. Those skin tones, which spanned the dusky rainbow from rose brown to plum black, all seemed to be draining of color. It felt as if we were in a segregated waiting room. For Coloreds Only. As if some Jim Crow virus had descended on our town, leaving us weak and sun-bruised.

As I toyed with the drawstring of my jacket, a blue windbreaker that used to belong to Raymond, I turned to the television mounted above the reception area. The news program cut to commercial break and a familiar jingle filled the room. Youth Sap. I knew the commercial by heart. A smiling blonde with impossibly tight skin smiled as she held aloft a benign porcelain bottle. A dramatic narrator intoned:

Say goodbye to crow's feet and age spots with Youth Sap. Our special melanin-enhanced formula gives you a radiant, sun-kissed glow in just ten weeks. Uncover your true complexion today!"

As the commercial faded to black, my mind drifted to the night of the fire. Two weeks had passed since my mother walked in our front door with soot in her hair. The fire was still being investigated, but initial reports blamed the blast on some type of compound in a new formula bottled at the plant. Who knew melanin was an accelerant? I was sixteen then, nearly seventeen, and studying chemistry. I knew melanin was a powerful polymer, protecting our skin and eyes against high temperatures and biochemical threats. A coveted pigment. But what happened if melanin became toxic, somehow poisoning the darker skins it was designed to protect?

That question plagued me as autumn worn on. I could no longer sleep in my bedroom, which faced the east side of the street, gazing into the baleful eye of morning. Even though I hid beneath my blanket when I went to bed, I slept fitfully. Sometimes my arm or cheek would be left uncovered during the night and I awakened to blisters cropping up on my skin like mushrooms.

Mother fared much worse. In a month's time, she had aged ten years. New wrinkles formed on her skin daily, it seemed. We abandoned our bedrooms and hunkered down on a worn sectional in the basement. Raymond's surliness turned to shock as he watched us deteriorate. Yet, he never came down with the flu that affected Mother and me and so many other women. Our sun-sickness grew so bad that my brother had to buy tarp and nail it above every window in our row house. Mother and I stumbled through those small dark rooms like feeble vampires too brittle to hunt for human blood.

Sandy was still gone. She simply vanished, as if she had drifted into some Bermuda Triangle at the end of the block. It was possible that my addled neighbor had wandered nearly three miles to the outskirts of Wing, down to the bottling plant, the night she disappeared. No one really knew where she went on her daily walks. Had she somehow fallen prey to the melanin bottlers?

I shuddered beneath my comforter, envisioning the gruesome brewing process. Did anyone really know how Fair Industries isolated the molecules that gave Youth Sap its anti-aging properties? The company had only been around for a few years. Maybe they kidnapped black women and girls, threw them into a giant vat in the basement of the factory, boiled their skins and extracted pigment that way.

It was a possibility.

Wing was small, but I didn't know every black family that lived within those forty-four blocks. Teen girls could vanish, assumed to be runaways. Single women could go missing, especially those considered "not right in the head." Unaccounted for and unmourned.

I toyed with my kitchen, as I often did when I was nervous. Those gnarled strands at the nape of my neck were kinkier than usual. I didn't have the energy to comb my hair or wash it. Mother had woven my hair into two uneven French braids the day we went to the clinic. That was weeks ago, and I still hadn't untangled them. Now I played with that matted nape hair, ripping a few strands out completely, as I thought back to the night of the explosion. Mother had come in the door, shaken and soot-laced. And I hugged her. Maybe the blast at the melanin factory had been radioactive.

I mulled over the question that troubled me that entire sunless fall: Could melanin become toxic? Could some type of contamination occur during the separation process, one that was passed from dark woman to dark woman, from brown girl to brown girl, like a plague? Maybe the night of the conflagration a batch, churning with the weight of its tainted mission, exploded and embers drifted up from the bowels of the factory, up from the heat-shattered jars of sap, and out into the night air, where the breeze carried them south, to our side of town.

Maybe Sandy was the supernova.

My mother cried out in her sleep, making me jump. I felt a rush of love for her and a need to protect her. But I didn't know how. I thought I was onto something, but who would believe me? There was no one with whom I could share my theories, wild as they were. The police would just dismiss me as a lonely kid who watched too many scary movies.

The coming days brought so many things to worry about. I worried about facing a life without sunshine. I worried about missing school. I still hadn't taken my SATs and didn't know when I would be well enough to finish studying. I worried about my wounded skin and mother's frailty. During the day, when she should have been working at the mill, she told me stories of her childhood.

"This feels like rheumatic fever," Mom said as she sipped tea from her end of the couch. It was actually a concoction of boiled garlic, honey and ginger to combat the "flu," and the room was pungent with the vapors of her tonic.

When Mother was seven, she had come home from school feeling light-headed and collapsed at the bottom of the stairs. Her father had to carry her up to her bedroom. Doctors still made house calls back then, and the family physician, a gruff Irishman named MacGregor, diagnosed her with rheumatic fever. For the next year, she lay in bed until the disease ran its course.

"Left me with a heart murmur," she said staring at the gray canvas hanging from the window, blotting out the light. "I felt hot, tired all the time. Blisters like these. Rashes."

I fingered the nodules that lined my own arm and face. Planets of thickened skin, a cosmos abandoned by a mutinous sun. "Did you think you were going to die?" I asked.

Mother blew into her teacup. Nestled there in the blanket, her skin ashen and furrowed, she looked like a little old woman in a nursing home waiting for an attendant to wheel her to a brighter place. "No," she said after a few moments. "My mother prayed for me every day. At the foot of my bed. On her knees. She wouldn't let me die. And I won't let us die either."

She said it with such authority that I believed her. Yet my body seemed beyond supplication. Little did I know, bleaker days were ahead.

One morning in late October, I was jolted awake. Dawn crept beneath the tarpaulin at the window like a dark rose, spilling wilted petals on the floor. Something felt wrong. Off. Even more so than usual. The basement was blurry. A haze surrounded the coffee table and the television that I couldn't blink away. I wiped sleep from my eyes trying to focus, but that fuzzy outline remained.

"Mom!" I cried, throwing off the blanket.

I heard her shift wearily from her side of the couch. "What's wrong, Enuma?" she said in a small voice.

"I'm going blind."

"You ain't going blind, baby. Just sick. We both are. It'll pass."

Mother's words did little to comfort me. Maybe they were more to comfort herself. There was no money for an eye doctor. She'd lost her part-time job at the phone company from missing so many days of work. Because she'd been employed at the textile mill for a dozen years, there was more security. But her sick leave was unpaid. There was no disability insurance for a prolonged "fever" that caused her skin to grow wrinkly.

In the coming days, as my vision waned and I lay in the blackness of the basement, I focused on sound. The stoic plink of water in the sink next to the washing machine. The cawing of birds perched on the telephone wire, taunting us with their fearlessness and their song. What struck me most was the absence of rhythm, a communal cadence of folks laughing on stoops and little girls skipping hopscotch, their shoes thudding against the sidewalk as they leapt from chalky square to chalky square.

If I focused on this sound with all my strength, could I convert it into light? Freshman year, I had watched Mr. Roth, my science teacher, perform an experiment with a transistor radio, a nine-volt battery and a tiny roseate bulb, which was unlit. As he switched on the radio and the upbeat synth-tinged sound of the Psychedelic Furs filled the room ("Ghost in You," I think it was), he ran a cable from the radio to a wooden board contraption housing the tiny lightbulb. A wavy "Oooh" sounded through the science lab as my classmates and I watched the diode flicker to life and gleam with a fixed fuchsia brightness.

"Audio signals can be transmitted in radio waves through space and in electrical currents through wire," Mr. Roth explained with a satisfied smile. "But not everything is as rosy as it seems, class. When one form of energy is transformed into another, some loss can occur."

Melanin was a conductor not only of light, but of sound. Or so it was thought. At least, that's what the men who congregated on the steps of the Masonic lodge down the street believed. I had passed that blue-and-white building on my way home from the bus stop many an afternoon and sometimes heard the masons discussing Africa and the superiority of dark skin, how we were like walking radios, more sensitive to various frequencies in the environment than our white counterparts.

What if my skin, ruined and sunless, could absorb all the sounds around me – the plinking water, cawing birds, the garlicky snores of my mother, even the empty hum of a street scrubbed clean of music – to become a superconductor, much like Mr. Roth's science experiment, until my body vibrated with the force of those audio waves and emitted a glow strong enough to chase away the shadows in the basement, bright enough to rival the deceitful sun?

I closed my eyes as firmly as I could and concentrated. I lay there, beneath my comforter squinting, tight, so tightly, until my head trembled and my neck muscles bulged and my heart raced. Swallowing sound. I tried to channel all the frequencies in my environment, every particle of noise, every little mote of melody, and slam them against the cement walls of the basement until they exploded to life like a galaxy on fire. My own private Big Bang. I focused until I got a headache, but no light emanated behind my closed lids. Mother whimpered in her sleep. I opened my eyes.

I often thought of Sandy.

After Raymond finished his chores and cooked dinner each night, he shared the local gossip. Sandy still hadn't returned. A few weeks after she disappeared, someone tacked "Missing" posters to the telephone poles on our street, and they still flapped there. Unanswered. Other families in our neighborhood had nailed tarp to their windows as well. Most of the girls from our side of town were still absent from school. The men on the block speculated that some new outbreak of Legionnaire's disease had struck Wing. It had been forty years since the first epidemic rampaged a convention of white men celebrating the nation's bicentennial in Philly, which was only six miles to the southeast. What in the world did the women and girls in my neighborhood have in common with the Legionnaires? I listened to my brother's stories, saying nothing, thinking of radioactive bottles of melanin. Compact porcelain graves.

Thanksgiving neared, ushering in a joyless season. Mother loved to cook and during the holidays, our tiny row house bulged with the smell of collard greens simmering on the back burner, sweet potato pie heavy with nutmeg and vanilla, and turkey browned to perfection. This Thanksgiving would be quiet. My mom was still bedridden and Raymond only knew how to make soup and fish sticks. There would be no waves of feminine energy bouncing around the kitchen because my aunts and other women family members were housebound as well.

After months of being confined to the basement, I'd had enough of darkness and musty air. Mother and I were like jars of preserves rotting in a cobwebbed cellar – sealed away in a prison that leeched our sweetness and toughened our skin. I needed air. A quick walk down the block. Anything. I hadn't been outside in so long but I needed to do something to escape my blanket and those covered windows. I would go out at night when my brother came home. I felt safer with the moon, with the icy brilliance of stars.

Against Mother's protests, Raymond helped me up from the couch and led me upstairs, through the kitchen and living room and over to the front door. He held my wrist with one hand and opened the screen door with the other. As the cool night air rushed in, I braced myself against some stinging sensation, some further assault on my skin. There was none. I took two or three steps across the threshold, holding the railing as I stood on our stoop.

"I got you, Enuma," my brother said, as I hesitated on the bottom step. His concern would have been touching a few months ago, even a little humorous. Now it just served to buttress my growing fear of incapacity.

The street was as dark as the basement and just as blurry. I strained to make out the shapes of the bushes in our front yard, of the row houses across the street – squat and uneven – of the trees that dotted the block. The air smelled sweet, sweeter than I remembered. I lowered myself on the step next to Raymond, listening to the night. As we sat in silence, I thought of the many nights Deirdre and Lisa congregated on their stoops, blasting hip-hop from radios, as I sat near the open window of my bedroom, listening to Bruce Springsteen and Billy Joel. Alone. They thought I was corny. I thought they were brash. A ravine separated us, a dusty gorge of misunderstanding, now piled high with regret.

Now that I yearned for community, there was no one around.

I thought of Billy Joel and the dying factories in his song "Allentown," which was twenty minutes away. I thought of the restlessness that buckled the sidewalks of my small town, where a bright girl once left on scholarship and returned a babbling shell. I thought of the girls who would never leave, and I was beginning to accept that I might be included in that company, girls who would never know other sidewalks, other cultures, other songs. A zoned life. They floated along the borders of Wing, like the cloudy waters of the Schuylkill that lapped at its banks, the "skulking river," aptly named by Dutch settlers, littered and forlorn. I thought of Bruce Springsteen and the hunger in his lyrics and his desire to dance in darkness. Eventually, he and Billy Joel left their hometowns. They always could.

As if sensing my sorrow, Raymond put his arm around me. The chilliness of the stoop pressed through my pajama bottoms. I was able to make out swaths of darkness in the windows of my neighbors' homes, a glassy blackness made even more prominent by the streetlight. Tarp. I closed my eyes as I leaned on my brother's shoulder. Come June, he would enlist in the Army, as our father, uncle and grandfather all did. Military men. Raymond worried about leaving Mother and me in our condition, and I sensed the heaviness of that decision resting on his shoulders. We sat in silence, mulling over our respective burdens. His could be remedied. Mine could not.

Into the stillness came the faint slap of feet on pavement. I sensed a brightness outside my closed lids, like the return of a contrite sun.

"The hell!" Raymond pulled away from me as he hurried to his feet. I opened my eyes, reaching for his arm. He helped me stand.

She moved down the block, down a sidewalk that knew her footfalls better than her father ever could, trapping them in stone like a wayward heartbeat. Sandy.

She was no longer the wrecked track star, pacing up and down the streets of our town, wearing a raggedy 'fro and short shorts. Her movements were determined. Sure. Her hair was gone. She was naked. Shimmering. No. Glowing. As if she had stood beneath the fiery geyser from the explosion at the melanin factory until she absorbed all the embers, thick with a pigment both dreaded and beloved, until a sun pulsed beneath her dark skin. The very eye of heaven.

I beheld her nakedness, marveling at her smooth head, the silky brown skin that gleamed with a dark luminosity, like a dying star whose light is barely discernible from Earth but which its own galaxy knows is both massive and divine. Where had she been? Why had she returned after being lost for so long? Had I inadvertently summoned her with my experiment in the basement, gathered her from the dust like a forlorn god craving companionship, fashioned in her own image and song?

Sandy headed toward her house in a sparkly shuffle, her newfound radiance competing with the street lamps. She was humming. She paused at the end of the walkway that connected our stoop to the sidewalk. Raymond grabbed my hand as if he feared some gravitational pull might yank me from the steps and over to her side.

Sandy gazed at me as if seeing me for the first time. Her grin was wide and knowing.

"Come," she said.

I shrugged off Raymond's hand and walked down the stoop. I didn't need my brother's help now. Even though the night was cool, the sidewalk felt warm beneath my bare feet as I headed toward Sandy. I didn't know if she was toxic, if my skin would bubble beneath her finger. But I did know that in a community of blistered, sun-broken women, I needed her phosphorescence. She stood in front of me. Pulsing. A firefly loosed at last from a jar. I followed her up the street.

After School Special
Tyhitia Green

Maggie shuffled down the sidewalk on her way home after school, lugging her backpack. Mom had told her that she should surprise the family with dinner one day. Cooking didn't appeal to her. It wasn't something she ever wanted to learn, especially at twelve years old. Easy breakfast food, yes. Nothing major. She looked forward to volleyball. The tournaments, the traveling, the fun. Cooking would remain her parents' duty if she could help it.

Besides, her dad had told her not to touch the stove again until she took cooking seriously. He got so mad with her when she burnt the food once. She told him it was no big deal, but he yelled anyway. Maggie got angry, too, and she threw the casserole dish and broke it. She had her dad's temper.

Mom grabbed both their shoulders. "You two are way too explosive when you become angry. Calm down before you destroy the kitchen." Maggie had been banned from the kitchen for two weeks.

She kept a brisk pace, even though her back buckled a little from the weight of the backpack. No friends walked home with her from the school bus. With the exception of Mrs. Abraham, most neighbors worked during the day, which didn't matter because she wasn't a baby. Her family had only lived in South Carolina for about two years, but they were comfortable and liked where they lived. Before now, they lived in a two-bedroom apartment in California. Mom and Dad wanted a change of scenery and a "real" home.

An engine roared as a truck puttered along the street past Maggie. She'd seen the white truck pass by when she stepped off the school bus. The same truck had driven through her neighborhood for the past week. No one paid attention to it, but she did. She knew all of her neighbors' vehicles. Luxury cars, mid-size sedans, minivans, and sports cars filled their driveways. That truck didn't fit and never stopped at any house.

The truck slowed down, and for about two solid minutes, the truck paced her every step. She refused to make eye contact and only walked faster, her sneakers scraping along the sidewalk. *Eye contact will only encourage a whack job, her mom would say.*

Maggie's heart raced, almost bursting through her chest like a bullet.

"Hey there," the man said. He put the truck in park, the engine idling, and leaned across the seat as he spoke.

She swallowed the lump in her throat. Maggie turned her head toward the truck and stared.

"Sorry to bother ya," he said, smiling with straight, white teeth. His cropped blond hair had too much gel. "But do you know where Ms. Sally Jackson lives?"

Mom told her not to talk to anyone she didn't know, so she shook her head no.

"Okay," he said, placing his hands onto his steering wheel. "Thanks. I'll just try to call her again."

He drove away and turned onto another street. The writing on the side of the truck read *Bill's Carpeting and Flooring*. A picture of a beige carpet sat on one side of the script, and a picture of a polished, hard wood floor on the other.

Breathing a sigh of relief, Maggie continued home. *Maybe he's not a weirdo, just really stupid? Who would try to find a customer's house for a week? It was the same truck, it just didn't have the writing and pictures before.*

The entire situation seemed odd to her. Mom talked about some TV show from when she was a child called After School Special. She said it was a show about warnings and special life lessons that helped kids deal with difficult situations and make well-informed decisions. Stranger Danger must have been in at least one of those episodes.

Home at last. Pine and bleach hit her in the face when she opened the door. Then, the urge to go to the bathroom kicked in, and Maggie dumped her backpack on the floor and ran upstairs.

After she dried her hands, an eerie feeling hit her in the stomach. When she opened the bathroom door, he was there, standing in the hallway between her and her bedroom, wearing the same smile. If they had a stupid alarm, she would have known he was there and could've done something. He was too well dressed to raise the neighbor's attention. No one would've suspected foul play from a slim, well-dressed white dude in a blue designer suit and polished black shoes. Maggie hadn't noticed his outfit before because she only looked at his face. If she had, she would've known something was wrong with this guy.

She snapped out of her stupor and spoke. "Wha—what, are you doing in my house?" She slipped out of the bathroom and inched away from him.

"I just came to say hello, Maggie." He flashed his teeth again.

Her stomach dropped. "What do you want? And how do you know my name?"

The guy stepped back, shrugging his shoulders and turning his palms upward. "I thought I'd stop in and say hello." He nodded toward the window in the guest bedroom. "Mrs. Abraham told me your name. Real easy to chat up. Oh…" As he reached for the dozen roses on the wooden table, the smell of his cologne wafted through the air and burned her nose. "Here."

What the hell? Does this pervert think we're on a date? "Please, just go." Maggie stifled a cry and backed away from him. "I won't tell anyone you were here."

He laughed and extended his hand. "By the way, I'm John." When Maggie stepped closer to the hallway bookcase, he came forward and grabbed her arm. "Uh-uh, you aren't going anywhere," he said.

"My parents will be home soon."

"Nah. Your parents won't be home for hours."

Her heart pumped so hard that blood rushed through her ears. Her hands shook and John's eyes widened.

"Wow," he said and smiled, pulling her into her bedroom. "I've never had dark meat before. You are just too pretty." She kicked him in the shin and he grunted. "Don't fight, just do what I say and I won't kill you."

He pushed her onto the bed and she sprung back up, sizing up the sicko approaching her. She reared back, jumped up, and spiked him in the nose.

John grabbed his nose and doubled over. Maggie dove to his left. He caught her leg and she stumbled before regaining her footing. She dashed for the bathroom and slammed the door shut seconds before he could reach her.

"Open the door, you little bitch," he shouted and pounded the door. "Now, you're starting to piss me off. I'm gonna tear apart that pretty little face."

She said nothing.

He slammed into the door and it cracked a little. Maggie snatched her cell phone out of her pocket to call the police. It was dead. *I forgot to charge it!* She looked around and regretted telling her parents that she hadn't wanted a window in her bathroom. Searching for a weapon, Maggie spotted a pack of razors her dad used. What would she do, shave him to death? The blades were too small to harm him.

Another crack. Any minute he'd break through and she'd have to defend herself. Mom had never prepared her for an attack like this. Her face grew hot with fear and rage.

The final crack caught her full attention. She braced her shoulder against the door, knowing her petite frame wouldn't be enough to stop him from forcing his way in. Wood splintered and the doorjamb snapped. The door swung open and she stumbled backward. John panted in the doorway, the smile gone. Maggie backed away, searching for something to use against him. She remembered her mom had left a bottle of bleach behind the toilet and she darted for it. He caught her before she could grab the bleach, snatching a fistful of her braids and pulling her out of the bathroom.

She screamed and he covered her mouth. "Shh," he whispered in her ear, dragging her back into her bedroom. "You're a fighter. I like that." He pulled at her shirt, biting his bottom lip in anticipation.

She struggled and bit between his thumb and forefinger. He slapped her and she fell on the floor. Blood leaked from her split lip.

He straddled and choked her. "I prefer you awake, but I'll take you unconscious."

She bucked and he squeezed tighter. As he reached for her belt buckle, an electric surge shot through her body. Something she'd never felt before. Her heart thumped against her breast-bone and anger drowned out her fear. Mom had told her that if she got too angry she could hurt someone. This was the angri-est she had ever been.

The perplexed look on the pervert's face gave her time enough to act. She snatched his hand away from her throat and twisted until it snapped at the wrist. "Get off me!"

John screamed and his eyes watered. His chest heaved in and out as he held his injured wrist at his side.

Maggie decided not to run. She lunged at him, sending him into the nightstand. She stomped his kneecap, which echoed the sound of a cracked walnut.

He screamed and grabbed his knee. "A little girl isn't this strong," he said and then passed out.

Maggie leaned down and grabbed his wrists. The one she broke had already begun to swell, and the bone moved around quite a bit. He awoke with a moan. "Where are you taking me?"

"Downstairs. I'm going to make my mom proud today."

His head hit the first step with a loud thud and he started to convulse. He tried to kick at her with his good leg, but she never lost her grip. Mom was right, she could do anything she set her mind to.

When they reached the bottom of the stairs, he whimpered. "Please. I'm sorry. Just let me go."

"I can't do that."

"Why?"

"You're helping me get dinner ready."

Maggie dragged him onto the kitchen floor and dumped him beside the refrigerator, then reached for the wall behind the oven. She pressed the black metal button and their standard oven popped out like a drawer, revealing a much larger stainless-steel oven in a beige tiled wall.

Pushing the faux oven out of the way, she pressed her palm into a metal slot that read her handprint, causing the gigantic oven to preheat. She grabbed a few spices from the cabinet.

Crawling toward the island, John tried to pull himself up. "You're dead."

"And you're dinner!" She sprinted after him.

He reached up far enough to grab a blade from the knife block atop the island and he swiped at her. She stumbled backward and he fell on her, slicing her face. A sliver of skin hung from her cheek, but there was no blood on the blade. Uninjured, she head-butted him in the nose and blood and mucous sprayed across his face. John stared at her face. He screamed, got off her, and backed away. Maggie stomped his other knee, cracking it. This time, a wet sucking sound accompanied the break. He howled in agony and passed out again.

Maggie moved her hair away from her face and took a quick glance at her reflection in the oven door. Mom would be really mad. It took lots of time to perfect the synthetic human skin.

While the man was out, she removed vegetables from the refrigerator. She cleaned and seasoned them like her mom taught her. She also hog-tied him.

Grunting and gasping interrupted her work. "What are you?" John whimpered.

"A girl." The gash revealed her slick charcoal skin. "Well, not a human one. You ruined this skin. Mom will be mad that she will have to fix this on a school night." She removed the artificial skin from her face, checking her eyes for damage. The elongated slits were vertical and silver. Not the sort of thing she could show her friends.

"Let me go," he begged. "I won't tell anybody. I swear."

"Can't do that."

"You'll get caught. People will look for me."

Maggie shook her head. Her dad would get rid of the truck. That's what he'd done with the other meals... guests. And no one even filed missing person's reports for them. She giggled and grabbed him by the nape of his neck. He struggled but only tired himself out. "We only eat bad guys, and no one really misses those."

She dragged him into the bathroom off to the rear of the kitchen. Steam enveloped the room as she filled the tub with hot water.

John swallowed hard, his Adam's apple bulging as he did so. "Look, look, okay. You don't want to eat me. I have a few diseases and you don't want to catch them."

Maggie smiled. Human diseases didn't affect them.

His eyes grew large and his breathing raspy. His breathing concerned Maggie. "I guess I'll set the oven lower."

He began shaking. Reality was setting in. "What? Why?"

She sighed. "You'll cook slower." She couldn't have him die before mom got home. What if she got the recipe wrong and mom needed to change something? She'd have to tend to the ugly business of scooping out some unnecessary parts and stuffing vegetables in them. She'd have to sew up some areas so he wouldn't bleed out. Blood would ruin the flavor.

But first, Maggie needed to shave him, so she grabbed a razor from dad's utility drawer. He yelped and begged as she shaved his back. She grinned and said, "Mom is going to be so proud that I got over my frustration and made dinner myself."

By the time mom got home, Maggie had already cleaned the bathroom and the kitchen, with the main course already in the oven. After the initial screaming, she'd had to place an apple in his mouth. Mom smiled and placed her pocketbook on the kitchen counter. "Wow, what's that smell?" She threw her hands in the air after noticing her daughter's face. "Oh Maggie, what did you do?"

Maggie's heart raced. "I just thought I'd surprise you guys with dinner."

"Your face!" mom said and examined her. "I'll have to make time to fix this tonight. You ought to be more careful, honey."

"It wasn't me," she said, glancing over at the oven.

John rocked back and forth, trying to get her mom's attention.

"Oh my goodness," Mom said, walking toward the oven.

"How'd I do?" Maggie shrugged. "I didn't do anything wrong, did I?"

Mom touched the glass oven door with one hand and rubbed Maggie's back with the other. "You did great, honey," she said smiling. "You got white meat. It's my favorite."

Therapies for World's End

Stefani Cox

I.

A journey becomes a journey before destination appears.

Sometimes it takes three years. Three years of desiccated food scraps, of retching and trying to keep stale bread and cheese rinds down, of dark skies and rubble sifted, always in dreaded hope of finding a familiar face.

Three years ago, I lost my mother. She disappeared into the darkness one night for a late water collection—I should never have let her leave alone. I knew she was gone by the pit of my stomach, which has yet to fail me in divining the truth of another's fate. I already knew this was the type of disappearance from which she would not return.

Now, I would take a bit of clothing, a flash of a near-lost memory, a whisper escaping crumbled brick. Instead, I have the silence that descended after all the electronics died. That particular quiet is mixed with the keening that continually permeates the air left around us.

We outside of formal homes are called survivors; I don't know what the others are named. The ones inside safe and warm during the evening hours don't need a label it seems. They get to be themselves as they are, which is by and large white and well-off.

My hands are ashed unrecognizable. I think I am still brown underneath, but I cannot be sure. I may now also be dust. Before the dust I was walnut-like, though I have never loved explaining my appearance in terms of food. Eat or be eaten has a new meaning toward the end of the world, and I don't want to be associated with the latter.

Dust people. We are everywhere. Clinging to the cities that no longer sustain us, to the remnants of buildings that have been shaken to their core and beyond that limit too. It was not one quake but a series of massive tremors and their hideous aftershocks that leveled most of the West Coast cities. A chain reaction of the most unimaginable kind.

The rumbles coincided with natural disasters of other types that were already pulling apart the country and the rest of the world. Wildfires, torrential storms and flooding, tornadoes, tsunamis. We were being ripped to shreds long before the economic hubs of the country collapsed.

What we yearn for now is water that can be drunk without a pill to kill the illness, for the gentle animals of our mothers' youths—and for their stories we were too impatient to listen to, the ones we now kick and shame ourselves for forgetting.

We desire cool loam soil. Rainbows after showers. Atmospheres of heavens before.

And touch that is soft.

No one knows how to make love anymore. We rut and strain like dogs when the need overtakes our better thinking. And then we scuttle away, alarmed that prolonged proximity might force us to see each other too clearly. Not one of us can handle that.

I am still a woman. Am I? I think so, though I rarely bleed, my body conserving precious nutrients without asking my input. Avoiding the ritual of scrounging for padded materials doesn't bother me too much.

Still, it is this body, my growing separation from it that finally makes me leave, head for the only trees left, the only forest within hundreds of miles that has managed to survive humanity's onslaught of extraction and destruction. I suppose my bones and matter are as good enough a reason to go as any.

Well, that and the roaches—for they remain kings of the city.

II.

My parts are a farce of limbs, of the way flesh should work.

My head is the most apparent, a buzz of circular thoughts and pink mush that forces its way against vision and sound. It rings and hums for my attention more insistently than anything else. It is stuck on high alert, with no way to come down.

I turn this way and that trying to see and hear the invisible.

My arms, when I sense them, are unbalanced—a pair of pendulums swinging to uneven rhythms. The good one, left, is my knife to cut through brambles and vines that sting me back. The other spins tiny circles at my side. Ripples left over from one of the medicines doctors give everyone now for panic.

My pelvis is a basket of needles. My stomach a river of acid. My toes, my ankles, my wrists, my neck, all voice their own complaints. I've given up trying to appease my aches and pains. I ask only that my body continue to carry me, as far as it can. For the most part, it acquiesces, even if the cold mornings make everything creak like a rusty train getting started on bad tracks.

My legs are a mystery, hobbling forward of their own accord. They go when the timing seems right to them, and they stop when the walking should be done. I can't sense them any better than the rest of my body, yet they power me toward a source I have never encountered, one I desperately need.

III.

What is a healer?

Is she the one who cures, who holds the stamina for life and dispenses of it forthwith?

Is she a sanctuary, a container for pain?

Others often think so, and she sometimes obliges, because it is true that one who cures must witness suffering—both her own and others'—to exist.

In this age what does healing consist of?

Does anyone still hold the road map to "better?" And if so, do the keys work in the ignition of the vehicle with which to travel the path?

All healers have an origin story, usually beginning with a rock or a tree or a river. A source of amalgamation, transformation, rooting. The thing that shapes her into later form. (Those who do not know wiser say *final* form.)

However you may define such a woman, be graced in her presence, and if you should happen on two or three at once, this is ascension.

I wandered into the forest blind of direction. And suddenly, a coalescing of brown bodies, clear eyes. Community.

IV.

The one who reaches down to me is an angel.

The ferns behind her body form a set of wings; the edge of sunset lingers as a halo. Slivers of angry reds and oranges prick at her, and I worry the shards will embed.

She is tall, but strong, the type who might have been chosen for sports at an earlier time. Her spiraled locs curl around her ears and down to her chin. Her eyes hold me even more tightly than the hand she has extended. She pulls me up.

I notice women all around her amidst the greenery, waiting patiently. A blue-black shoulder here, a tan exposed waist there, a twinkle of eyeglasses from one to my right. They wear leaves and hides, their clothing is made of it—brassieres fitted to ample chests and wide, short skirts threaded together with vines.

Until the angel speaks, I do not recognize any of them as human. But what she says floats from her mouth in words I understand.

You need us.

There is nothing in her statement to argue with, and I realize my purpose has always been to find them.

V.

Healing is not what I think it is.

Though I did not know my goal, I have dreamt of flowers, of roses and light and sweet lavender sprinkled past my nose.

It isn't that healing is *not* these things. Only that they are extras, side characters to the protagonist, the main star, my pain. The knot of everything that has happened to me these past years and beyond, perhaps everything that has happened to our people together through time.

This is the material they work with. They lay me down in the center of their circle, a patch of moss, when I had no idea such a cushion still existed. It is a luxury my senses immediately try to reject. *There is no time for this. You should be finding food, not lingering with strange women on the forest ground.* I do my best to ignore the thoughts.

The moss is the only calm as the healers begin and my body shudders and spasms, trying to hold onto the fierce, jagged pieces, my grotesque attempt at a whole in this wild. They have been as precious to me as children, these parts that I have nurtured with all their dysfunctional qualities.

Here those pieces have to come free—the women demand it. They call my anger to them, the rage and irritations that often shove me toward my own destruction. They pull strings of the stuff to the surface of my skin, like a latticework cage of threads.

They call my sadness next, and I am not surprised at its torrents, an energy just as powerful that materializes to me as a flow of waters. The waves rush to fill gaps in my net of fury.

But when they coax forth my fear, that is where I worry I will break. They hesitate. They sense how much I have needed to deny, to bury this part of me. They wait for my heaving chest to slow, for the trails of snot sliming my face to lessen. And when I am ready, they pull.

They drag opposite, somehow perfectly balanced in a tug-o-war, my body the red-taped middle. I am sure I will come apart at any moment to nothing.

They pull at my memories, and I scream for my lost mother, the hole that lives in my heart for never having found her body. I scream for our home that I could not hold down as a single woman, bulldozed mere weeks later for an ultra-rich development. I scream for myself, and I disappear into waves of shame at my inward focus.

Then, a prism of light. The rainbow I always wanted to see. I don't know where it has come from, where it ends, how I am experiencing it, where I am even. Only that it is a perfect wonder.

Among it all, their faces. Some hard, some gentle, all melanated. Their gazes holding me, refusing to let me deny the truth—

I have never been, and will never be alone.

VI.

I sense the shift before I open my eyes.

Their absence only in the physical terms I know to use.

I hold my lids shut a minute longer to remain in the place they have left me, not sure that I am strong enough to see beyond the dark. But then I hear a bird.

Not just any bird, a songbird trilling the three-note series from outside my bedroom window as a child. The tones that marked weekend mornings before chores or mandated volunteering from mother, who ran the neighborhood resource council and was forever planting trees and testing water aquifers. Then, I hated the intrusion on my schedule, the weight of obligation in an otherwise liberated day. Now, of course, I would trade everything for that quiet burden.

The bird's coaxing floats my lids open to the brilliant forest, this scarce glow of leaf-filtered sunlight. Scents of pine envelop my nose and mouth.

I expect to feel gloriously empty, no longer plagued by any emotion I don't want to feel. Instead I am raw, sensing all the healers have drawn forth still rushing and twisting through my skin. I am a kaleidoscope of feelings, the opposite of zero. And I cannot put my armor back on, hard as I try.

They have made me into one of them; I feel this transformed state. I am both myself and a servant now—dual truths residing in one small body, one brown shell of awareness. The newness stings. I am unaccustomed to being shaped, to being formed by hands not my own.

I want to shake my head to the air in confusion. I want to roar at the currents that make up my surface, at how they point me back toward the city, toward all the broken people I have run from. What the healers have done for me, I must learn to build with others now. I have completed a turn around the sun, redefined my place in this existence.

A journey lasts longer than a lifetime, the quest itself a practice of belief. We are beings to search and then wonder. We begin at the middle, and end where the roads never meet.

Carolina Anole

M. Shelly Conner

The truck, built for snow, appeared awkward on the Texan landscape. Although similarly sized as the *everything is bigger in Texas* vehicles, its demure rust spots betrayed age and time in a climate that encompasses the full range of the four seasons. "Why white folks always gotta live so far out?" Jean lamented.

Rachel shrugged, clutching the steering wheel against the dusty gravel. "Why you seem so surprised? Chicago housing has always been about black integration and white flight."

"Yeah, but this ain't Chicago."

"Still though." Rachel chanced removing her hand from the jumping steering wheel to briefly give her partner a comforting squeeze. "Still *people.*"

"*Some* people," Jean said.

"Right," Rachel agreed.

They fell into a familiar silence, each processing their experience, starting with their marriage and backtracking into separate paths of development. Jean went to school in the white town outside of Cleveland where hers was the only black family in town. She rehearsed the tenets that she had learned to follow when being the token: smile, shut the fuck up and don't take no shit. Jean actually thought her wife to be privileged, having grown up so steeped in blackness—black neighbor-hoods, schools and friends.

Rachel still felt trapped by her mother's accusation that her doctoral degree and new tenure-track post had assimilated her into useless blackness. *What good is higher education if it benefits and excludes the same folks as always?*

"This ain't our Texas." Jean cut the silence.

"Was Chicago any more ours?" Rachel asked, pulling their thoughts back to the previous year's Memorial Day weekend. After spending the holiday visiting family in Memphis, they returned to Chicago, exhausted from the eight-hour drive. They hurriedly unpacked the truck, and before they could exchange their travel clothing for pajamas or even pour a relaxing drink, gun shots split the night's silence so close to the house that they scrambled into the foyer away from windows.

Rachel had looked at Jean's face, tears streaked to her chin, and grabbed her hands. "I think we need to get down, love."

Down they sank, slowly and silently, as if the outside violence could hear the soft scrapes of their clothing rubbing the wall in their descent. As they lay sprawled on the floor, hands tightly clasped, Rachel promised, "We are going to get out of here."

When they awoke to find that their garage had been burglarized during their vacation, Rachel's resolve only strengthened. They had been skeptical of where Rachel should apply for jobs even in a highly-competitive market. But, they knew that Chicago no longer was the sweet home depicted in blues lore.

And when Jean returned from work on more than one oc-casion, trembling with rage and recounting tales of catcalls and men who trailed behind her polite no's even as she switched train seats, and her pleading eyes searched the downward gazes of her fellow passengers, Rachel calmed her wife with tea or television or card games or sex until Jean slept. Then, she crept from their bedroom and spent the twilight hours on writing samples, diversity statements, and research agendas.

Her research of the droves of blacks that escaped enslavement and joined the western expansion inspired the creative narratives that ultimately landed her current position, their Texas relocation, and their first social visit at the home of two of her new colleagues: Jack and Ginger.

"For real?" Jean said upon hearing their names.

"I know." Rachel frowned, keeping her eyes trained on the endless road. "Something just seems off about it. Like that time after undergrad when I was looking for work and found that ad in the paper." She looked at Jean, five years her junior and added, "You probably never had to apply for jobs from newspapers using fax machines."

"Did you ever get a job from a paper using a fax machine?" Jean asked.

"No, but I sure did apply to a bunch."

"What about fax machines and Jack and Ginger?" Jean reguided the conversation. "I also feel like I should be able to speak in ampersand just to say their names."

"Right?" Rachel chuckled. "I get to the training way out in bumblefuck Illinois for what turns out to be a door-to-door sales job where I gotta— turns out— shadow some white trainee as we visit houses that have Confederate flags flying. In Chicagoland."

Jean's side eye cut through Rachel's winding story. "Two things: whatever we encounter here, I'm far more equipped to deal with it than you. And what about Jack and Ginger and this long ass story you still haven't told?"

"Okay. The two dude bros in charge, and I mean early twenty-something—yeah, I was too, but I was applying for entry level and they were already *directors*."

Jean gave an exaggerated glare at her watch.

"Were named...drumroll please."

"Girl..." Jean rubbed her temples. "I'm not sure the payoff to this story is going to pay off."

"Chris Carter and Mark Snow."

Jean wrinkled her face. "I'm trying to get it. I am. Is it the initials? I want to feel you, Ray, but we are on a dirt road traveling into whatevers and I really just want to get to the punchline and laugh with you, baby."

"Those are the creators of the X-Files TV show." Rachel quickly shot an incredulous glace at Jean before snapping her head back toward the road.

"And?"

"And?" Rachel rolled her eyes. "I went in there and those two names together, the X-Files creative team and this ain't X-Files. I was like nawl." A series of snort clucks and teeth sucks punctuated Rachel's statement.

"Well, how 'nawl' could you be if you still did the shadow training and saw that Confederate flag?" Jean smirked.

Rachel pursed her lips. "I was an unemployed 'nawl' who had driven the hour and a half outside of Chicago, so I figured to give it the whole spiel. Anyway, we were selling coupon books.

"Wait, what?" Jean gasped. "I lied. This story keeps getting better."

Rachel sighed. "You wanna hold up the story or no?"

"I mean, we're moving more into the epic side of the story spectrum, but I guess it's about as long as this road we're on, so go on."

Rachel scanned the prairie around them and silently agreed as she continued. "Coupon books were basically a precursor of Groupon, but door to door. And me and this blond, walking around the sprawls of white flight, approach this one house with the largest Confederate flag. Or more accurately, we approach a huge Confederate flag with a house attached to it."

"Did y'all ring the bell?"

"Hell no. I mean, I stopped on the sidewalk. It was DNA instinct. You know science has found that trauma can carry on through DNA?"

Jean laughed. "So you needed slave ancestors tapping your cells to tell you to stay away from houses with Confederate flags?"

"Yeah, smartass." Rachel joined her wife's laughter, which ended with a customary hum and head shake.

* * *

The computerized GPS voice brought their thoughts current and Jean raised a mock toast. "May this be a regular boring mixer and not the weird, please don't touch my hair mixer." She sighed before adding, "I gotta find some place to get my hair done."

Rachel snickered. "Yeah, well, we'll just consult Google on that one." Their destination was announced as a small road to the right, and she slowed to make the turn, revealing a sprawling plantation-style home. "Remember the rules?"

Jean nodded. "Don't get political; don't get personal; don't get drunk...But, weren't you hired to have these conversations?"

"I was hired to have these conversations for them not with them. There's a difference. Let's just think about how long we're going to stay," Rachel suggested.

Jean thoughtfully replied, "What if it's actually fun?"

A pause preceded their in-unison answer. "An hour."

"And if it's fun, we don't want to overdo it," Rachel advised. "Save some fun for the next run." She slowly guided the truck onto grass populated by a range of luxury cars too clean to have made the same dusty road trip they had completed.

"Try not to get blocked in," Jean suggested.

Rachel nodded and tapped on the gas pedal to power through the dampness of the mud-caked grass. "Must have rained out this way," she muttered against the slight resistance of tires to the sucking ground. Satisfied with the truck's position, she switched off the ignition. Within seconds, the summer humidity engulfed them and they sprang out of the truck.

Jean slapped at her thigh exposed by her summer dress. "Goddamnit! These mosquitoes!"

"We've got spray in the truck. Let's do a quick once over."

Jean shook her head. "No, we'll be in the house soon and I don't want to smell like DEET 35 amid all this swankiness we're about to encounter."

They walked quickly, scattering small lizards in their wake. "Ugh, creepy crawlies!" Rachel shuddered.

"Just little geckos." Jean grabbed Rachel's hand. "They're more afraid of us."

"Oh, I doubt that." Rachel rushed them onto the pavement and slowed as they approached the sprawling white columns of the two-story building. "Damn, this place is huge."

A small lizard hovered near the doorbell before Rachel could press it. "I got it, love." Jean clapped her hands and the creature scattered just as the door opened, revealing their host and a glimpse of guests meandering around grandiose furnishings. "Well, hey y'all," he boomed. "We was wondering when y'all would make it through."

Rachel smiled and turned to introduce Jean before he interrupted, "Oh, come on in here. We do introductions inside. I know we're in the South, but we are civilized."

Once inside the spacious foyer, Rachel started again. "Jack, this is my wife, Jean."

Jack dramatically enfolded Jean's hands into his large, smooth manicured ones. "A vision," he gushed as his wife emerged behind him. Without removing his eyes from Jean, he said, "Ginger, my love, meet our most prized guests, Rachel and her lovely wife Jean."

Ginger wrapped an arm around her husband's waist and gave a gentle squeeze to Jean's shoulder, where her hand remained, creating an intimate circle between the two couples. "Oh, so lovely, and your hair..." She raised her hand toward Jean's braids and stopped short of contact. "Are these Senegalese braids?"

Surprised, Jean stammered, "Um, yes. Yes, they are." Her muscles began miniscule movements to re-establish personal space.

Ginger, with a final shoulder squeeze, released Jean and turned her attention to Rachel. "She's adorable when she's surprised. It's okay. We're more than just big steaks, big hats, and big hair." She patted her own blond coif before adding, "Jackie, why don't you show these ladies to the kitchen for appetizers."

They followed Jack through rooms filled with various versions of nondescript guests, arriving at a large, open kitchen streaming with natural sunlight from floor-to-ceiling windows.

"This is an amazing space, Jack." Rachel scanned every surface. A fleeting motion caught her eye from a corner. Blinking it into focus, she recognized a small lizard. Her breath quickened.

Jean struggled to interpret the change in her wife's demeanor, but added, "This is Rachel's dream kitchen."

"Well, y'all help yourselves to all the food. Let me grab y'all some drinks." Jack meandered through guests that seamlessly parted to make way for his exit.

"Don't. Eat. Anything," Rachel stressed. Her eyes glanced furtively, following blurs of motion that pinged around the house like lightning bugs in the night air. "Is it the same one?"

"What?" Jean asked, matching her gaze to Rachel's quickly changing targets until she spotted a lizard slinking against a baseboard. "Oh."

"I've counted like five so far," Rachel whispered as their hosts returned with two whiskey tumblers.

"Bourbon, if I recall." Jack beamed and raised his glass.

Ginger followed suit. "A toast, darlins, to a wonderful new friendship."

They accepted their drinks and toasted. Rachel diligently drained the contents and tried unsuccessfully to pry her eyes away from a bold lizard staring defiantly back at her. Jack followed her gaze.

Jean decided to address the elephant-sized lizard in the room. "So, um, are they pets? The lizards. We've seen quite a few."

Jack and Ginger smiled together as he answered, "Oh, lord no. Nothing so primitive. The anolis carolinensis are our closest neighbors. They're more like…"

"Friends," Ginger said as Jack nodded in agreement.

"Truer words, Ginger," Jack added. "They take care of all the pesky little insects around the house.

Jean found Rachel's hand and clutched it. "That'd be perfect for Rachel. She's got a phobia."

Rachel elbowed her. "Nooo. I wouldn't say a phobia."

Jack tilted his head. "Do tell!"

Rachel searched for a response as her trained eyes continued to scan her surroundings, made easier as fewer guests circulated in the room. "I just don't like bugs."

Jack raised a glass. "Well, here here. To no bugs!"

Rachel saluted with her empty tumbler. "Jean got bit by something nasty the other day."

Jean shot a side eye toward Rachel as her hand self-consciously rubbed the spot on her neck. "It's nothing."

Jack raised a hand toward her neck. "Oh, no. Would you mind?"

Jean nervously slid her braids away from the nape of her neck to reveal the small red bump. Jack trailed his index finger across it and clicked his teeth before shaking his head. "Ah, yes. The huntsman has been afoot."

Jean's brow furrowed. "Beg your pardon?"

Rachel wondered why the party seemed to be thinning out. She could easily spot the lizards now. Guests no longer blocked the view of the countertops. Only a of couple occupied seats where moments earlier, guests outnumbered chairs. She wondered where Ginger had disappeared to, having not noticed her departure from their conversation.

Jack continued, "The huntsman spider, non-toxic bite to humans. Prefers to dwell under rocks and such but occasionally will wander into a dwelling. I suspect your moving activities may have stirred him up." Jack completed his inspection and rubbed his fingertips.

Rachel snapped her attention back just as Jean responded, "Hydrocortisone."

Jack whipped a handkerchief from his pocket and carefully removed any trace of the ointment from his hand. "I see."

"Where's your restroom?" Rachel asked.

"There's one through those doors to the right and another at the top of the stairs."

"Excuse us." Rachel grabbed Jean's hand and scurried to the restroom on their level. Finding it locked, they speed walked their way through the few remaining guests and up the stairs. Rachel locked the door behind them and pressed her back against it. Her flushed face reflected in the mirror alongside Jean's concerned one.

"What the hell, Ray?" Jean twisted her braids.

"Have you noticed everyone seems to be gone? Not leaving, but gone?" Rachel whispered.

"Things are getting creepy here," Jean agreed. "Maybe they moved to other parts of the house?"

"Maybe, but I don't even see anyone moving about. It's like one minute there was a cluster of folks talking and the next...gone."

Jean whispered back, "I didn't notice."

"How could you not?"

"I don't know. I suppose I was distracted by your co-worker fingering my spider bite! I wasn't people counting." Jean scratched her neck. "So creepy."

"Well, you know what else I was counting?" Rachel leaned closer. "All those fucking lizards. They are everywhere."

Jean nodded. "I guess I was getting desensitized to them. I mean, I saw them but..."

Rachel placed her hands on Jean's cheeks and centered their eyes. "There's some weird shit going on and I think we should just leave."

"It hasn't been an hour," Jean protested. "Baby, this could just be, you know, your phobia. What if everyone is out by the pool? You know this place has got to have a pool."

Rachel shut her eyes. "I don't care. I don't care if I'm freaking out. I don't like how it feels here."

Jean gently kissed her wife's lips and forehead. "Okay, baby. We'll go. What do we tell Jack and Ginger?"

"We don't tell them shit. We just ghost. I'll make up something later about you not feeling well or something." Rachel paced and paused, lifting her gaze to a vent in the ceiling.

"Why me?"

"Shhh!" Rachel hissed and pointed toward the vent, where a faint tapping could be heard.

Jean grabbed her hand. "Let's get the fuck out of here."

They moved together in a halting manner unsure of fleeing or sneaking. Downstairs, they were greeted by Jack and Ginger. "Is everything okay?" Ginger asked as they stood in front of the exit.

"Yes, um…" Rachel stammered. She wondered if they'd have to fight their way out. She looked at Jack, every bit of the cliche middle-aged, former college athlete. Still solid in all the places that would count. And Ginger's sinewy yoga-class form. Rachel glanced at a silver tray of appetizers and silently began to countdown her attack. *Three, two…*

Without a word, Jean yanked Rachel and pushed past their hosts. Sprinting to the truck, they were certain of only one thing: their desire to escape. Inside the truck, Rachel fumbled with the keys in the ignition. Sweat instantly covered them in the sun-baked interior. Finally, the truck roared to life and Rachel threw it in gear only to find wheels spinning and mud flying. She jammed her thumb onto the four-wheel drive button and the truck instantly lifted itself from mire and skidded onto the driveway.

As Rachel peeled away from the house, Jean stared back through her side mirror. Through the vehicle's dust trail, she could just barely make out Jack and Ginger in the large picture window of the house, holding drinks with perplexed looks as the slightest tinge of green crossed their faces.

Cromartie Street

Kristian Astre

She'd been to six stores that hour, and not one of them had salt.

"What kind of shit is this?" she muttered to herself.

Rayon was semi-new to the Bronx, and first thought it was something as simple as not knowing where to look. Until the third store, anyway. After the fifth, she started imagining it some sort of mediocre conspiracy, a bored teenager's ploy to see to it that no meal north of Manhattan would consist of any flavor. But after the sixth, it was just funny. She was shaking her head while taming a modest giggle when she saw it, lit up on the neon green street sign like it was layered in highlighter. *Cromartie Street.*

There was nothing peculiar about the street name, it was that she didn't recall seeing it before. Rayon had been up and down that block several times, that day alone, and not once did she see a Cromartie Street. She looked down at her phone, and the street name didn't even register with Google Maps, so she knew something was up. She glanced down the road and saw mostly barren lots over taken by gnarled weeds and too bright dandelions, there were purple flowers too, small ones.

Rayon had no idea what they were, just that they were small, clustered, and inviting. The little flowers surrounded the only building Rayon could see occupying the block, a big box of a building with white signage above the front window laced in flashing rainbow lights. The words as jarring as the sign, "SALT HERE".

Rayon almost crept up to the building, expecting some oddly finagled apparition to jump out and scare her into oblivion. There was no door, just an open space under the sign and between the windows. She stuck her head in first, surveying the shop like the whole odd occurrence was something normal. The signage didn't lie, she saw salt immediately. It was all she saw. Rows and rows of salt lining every shelf in the store. Nothing but salt, and an oversized cash register. She stepped inside and moseyed over to the nearest shelf, picking up the first packet on the row. Rayon could have sworn that when she touched the salt a gust blew into the shop, knocking her high pony off to the side.

She heard the woman before she saw her, unsure of which would have caught her more off guard.

"Looking for salt," an old raspy voice echoed through the small space.

Rayon turned around and almost dropped the pack. Directly in the middle of the store stood a small, stout woman, head wrapped in a tan silk scarf and her body ornamented in matching drapery, water falling her silhouette. Her skin looked just as Rayon's father's once looked, smooth, cool, and a rich deep-seated brown – but the woman had moles, moles that resembled freckles. They were almost everywhere on her cheeks, chin, and in abundance on her forehead. The woman stepped closer to Rayon, extending her arms, motioning to the rows of product.

"Looking for salt?" she asked again.

"Oh," Rayon stuttered. "Yeah, I'll just grab this one."

The woman waddled to the register and Rayon followed down behind her. She placed the salt on the counter and the woman began to ring her up.

"Will you be needing a bag?" the woman asked.

"No," Rayon said while shaking her head. "I'm good."

The woman smiled, a beautiful smile. The kind that made the room and anyone in it light up. Rayon smiled back at her. It dawned on her that that was the first time she'd smiled that day, chasing salt was no smiling matter, even when it became laughable.

"How much is it?" Rayon asked.

The woman continued ringing her up, furiously pressing the old broken down buttons on the register.

The woman pursed her lips and gave Rayon an almost under eyed look before she said, "It's cheap, darling, just eleven strands…"

"Sorry," Rayon replied as she leaned in, assuming she heard incorrectly.

"Eleven strands," the woman annunciated.

"Strands of what?" Rayon asked.

The woman responded, "Hair, of course. That's the currency here."

Rayon looked at the woman like she was joking, low and behold, the woman's once beautiful laugh didn't reappear and all that was left was the under eyed annoyance.

"You want me to pay you in hair?" Rayon repeated.

The woman only nodded.

Rayon touched the tip of her freshly permed ponytail and stared at the woman staring at her.

"Is this a joke?" she questioned.

"No," the woman said. "Just the currency we take. You have plenty of hair, surely you can spare eleven strands."

The woman pulled out a pair of scissors from seemingly nowhere and slid them toward Rayon.

"You won't find salt anywhere else," the woman said lowly as she removed her hand from the scissors.

Rayon twisted her fingers over the strands, feeling each individual one roll atop her finger and thumbprints, settling along the grooves of her identity.

"What'll it be?" The woman sounded more annoyed now.

Rayon thought of turning around and leaving the salt on the counter. Saying screw the old lady and taking off out of the store; but then she remembered the six shops, and the time, and that if she didn't put the soup on in a few hours it wouldn't be ready the next day when her mother and sister were due. Rayon rolled her eyes and pulled the elastic off the top of her head. She grabbed a small bundle of hair and began piecing out a tiny section. She started counting then, one, two; the strands were soft and sharp, three, four; like a razor or edge of paper, five, six; but not so sharp they could cut her, seven, eight; just enough to remind her that her curls were gone, nine, ten; that they'd been tamed, eleven.

Rayon put her strands of hair on the counter and the woman scooped them up in a noticeable hurry. She pushed the salt toward Rayon and stuffed her hair deep into the open register.

"Thank you, darling," the woman said, motioning for Rayon to head toward the space between the windows.

Rayon winced a bit at the woman's abruptness, but picked up her salt and left. She had some soup to start on. After leaving the store, Rayon's walk shifted into a half jog as she hurried home. She had to get the beans on. It was her first year preparing the soup, the memorial soup if you will. It'd been eleven years and three hundred and sixty four days since her father's untimely demise, if we can really call death that. Rayon didn't know what killed her father, just that he didn't wake up after a nap one day. Her mother refused an autopsy, so that was that.

"He's gone," her mother said. "Cutting him open won't bring him back."

Every year on the anniversary of his death, Rayon, her mother, and sister Vy would come together for a day of remembrance and red pea soup, their father's favorite. This was Rayon's first year hosting the lunch, after years of trying to convince her mother. The last thing she needed was bland soup/a reason for her mother to never allow one of her daughters to cook for the family again.

She rushed up the stairs in her apartment building, the beat of reggaeton pulsing through the walls; she could feel the vibrations under her feet. They almost jolted her upwards and into the apartment, where she became winded, but flew into the kitchen and immediately added salt to the pot of low boiling beans on the stove. They'd stay like this overnight, before anything else would be added; the beef, peppers, and other seasonings. Only after Rayon salted the bean water did she realize her exhaustion. She'd been running around most of the afternoon in her quest for salt, and it had caught up to her. Rayon began stripping down before getting into her bedroom, first her black tank and then her favorite pair of tights. She always went underwearless, save her period week, as she wore pads instead of tampons due to a horrid toxic shock event when she was seventeen. That was over ten years ago, but it felt like yesterday to Rayon. Her bare body hit the bed and she sank into the comforter like it was the softest thing she could fathom. Before rolling off to sleep, Rayon ran her fingers over the small patch of pulled strands and hoped that the soup would be worth the new growth she'd be facing. Her phone began to ring, but she was asleep before the sound resonated with the rest of her.

The sun hit Rayon's back like fire on aloe, hot, sticky, and refreshing. She stood and stretched the way she did every morning, a half formed sun salutation. Rayon felt good this morning, not stiff and tight like she would most days after sleeping on her brick mattress. Her sun salutation wasn't so half-baked that morning, but fully formed. She jumped into the cold shower and washed the salty layer off her back, feeling every pore take a well needed sigh of relief. It was a cold shower, so there was no steam to wipe away off the mirror. Rayon stepped from behind the curtain and saw herself in a light she hadn't since, since ever. She stepped closer to the mirror and put her hand on her head, feeling nothing but the stubble of her recent strands. Her hair was gone. All of it. She began rubbing her head like it was an illusion, as though if she kept making contact her hair would suddenly reappear.

Rayon pulled the shower curtain back, no hair. She went into her room, not a strand in sight. It had just disappeared, and she was sure she knew who to blame. Rayon grabbed another pair of tights and a t-shirt before bolting out the door. She skipped about two steps at a time and took off out of the building. She was in a full sprint by time she touched the sidewalk, and she stayed that way until she neared *Cromartie Street*. Well, where Cromartie should have been. She looked around at the two streets paralleling the invisible Cromartie.

"What on earth," she said as she blew.

Rayon asked a few passersby if she was in the right area, they'd never heard of the street.

"And I've lived here since '72, though they'll try buying me out before '22!" one man exclaimed. "No Cromartie round here."

Rayon ran home and noticed how steady her breathing was, even as she climbed the multiple stories, she felt evened out. As if the air was being absorbed by the same pores that opened up that very morning. She felt reinvigorated in her angst. She got home and flopped down on her bed again.

"Damn that old obeah woman," Rayon mumbled under her breath.

She reached for her phone and saw them, the twelve missed calls from the night before. Stacy. She knew it before checking the call log, she was the only person Rayon knew that would call that many times without sending a text. There were no messages either, she'd send a text before she'd leave a voicemail. Big brother and all. She might have been the only person in Rayon's life that was happy about the Snowden stuff, because it meant she was right. Rayon had known Stacy for five years, they'd been an item for three. They broke up almost a year before, and attempted to stay friends with little success. She imagined the excuse this time would be the anniversary of her father's death, but if it wasn't one thing it was another, Rayon wanted the whole thing to stop. They weren't good for each other. The love was hard, and heavy and fluid; but so was everything else. The break up was Rayon's idea, and whenever she was asked what happened, there was never any definite answer – it just was. Rayon picked up the phone and rested her finger on the call button, but she swiped it away. Cold turkey, that's what they call it.

Rayon went into the kitchen and turned up the heat on the pot of beans, they had softened and the salt water had become the same burgundy shade as the beans. She added the rest of the ingredients to the pot and stirred the soup for nearly an hour. They'd be there soon, so Rayon set the table. This would also be her mother's first time seeing her new place; Vy had been over a few times before. She moved to the Bronx as a community organizer, to live with the people she worked for on a daily basis. Her mother didn't understand it, giving up a rent controlled apartment in lower Manhattan for space in a triplex so far out of the city; but Rayon didn't expect her mother to understand, she rarely did. There was a knock on the door.

"It's open," Rayon yelled.

Her sister pushed the door open to their mother saying, "You can't be so reckless Rayon, how on earth are you leaving the door unlocked like this?"

"Hey Ma," Rayon said as her sister joined her in the kitchen and hugged her neck.

"The hell happened to your hair?" her sister Vy asked.

Rayon rolled her eyes as she said, "Don't ask."

Their mother entered the kitchen, "Well, your hair comes as no surprise to me. Isn't that the next step?"

"Next step towards what, Ma?"

The room became quiet. Vy glanced at her mother as Rayon stared at her. Their mother sat down and motioned to her empty bowl.

"Soup…" their mother said.

Vy sat down next to her and Rayon began to share out the food. Their bowls were filled to the brim and Rayon joined them at the table. They didn't say grace on this day, the only day their mother didn't say grace, as their father didn't care much for religion. They sipped the soup, and remembered.

"It's good Ray," Vy said.

Rayon smiled at her sister. "Thanks. What do you think, Ma?"

Their mother nodded. "Good…a little salty, though."

Rayon felt what little hairs she had left stand up.

"Dad liked his soup cooked with flavor, Ma," Rayon said.

"I know," her mother replied. "I just think it's a little bit too salty."

"And I find yours bland," Rayon said. "You don't see me saying that though."

"Okay," Vy interjected. "Today is supposed to be about Dad, not us."

"How?" their mother asked, "by drinking soup?"

"No," Rayon snapped. "By trying to hold on to him."

Her mother put her spoon down and intertwined her fingers. "What do you have to hold on to? Duppie?"

Vy said, "Mom, please…"

"It's okay, Vy," Rayon said. "I'm trying to hold onto a memory Ma, do you know what that is?"

Rayon stopped listening. She felt herself lifting above the room, where she was floating and looking down at the conversation shift into an argument. She watched from the ceiling fan as so much inaudible anger took wind. As her mother threw blows about everything she couldn't stand about her: the apartment and soup and job and ex-girlfriend and newfangled baldness; and for the first time, Rayon's response. Her mother's judgmental nature, closed mindedness, bigotry, ignorance, and hella unsalted soup. Rayon was beginning to rage, and she watched herself morph into a person that was capable of it. The apartment looked different from that angle. She figured it would, but not that much. It seemed smaller, tighter, stuffy, and cramped. Which was odd, because the thing Rayon loved most about it was the light it let in, and all the space she had. Rayon floated down into her body, red eyes and a sore throat.

"We don't even know what happened to him," Rayon said. "If he suffered or not. How can you not care? Wasn't there any love there?"

Her mother stood and gave her an under-eyed glance. She headed for the door and said, "There still is, and always will be."

Rayon's heart stopped, or skipped a beat, one of the two. Their eyes met and locked on each other like they were seeing the other for the first time. Grief was funny that way, Rayon understood – like swimming against the current in the hopes of finding, of finding. Their mother left in a near huff and as Vy followed she looked back, grinning a soft grin only her sister could see.

"I like this Rayon," Vy winked and walked down behind their mother.

As the words fell off of her sister's lips, Rayon realized that she liked her too. She went to the bathroom and looked at herself again. Hairless and perm free. She ran her hand across her scalp, feeling the pricks of hair embed themselves into her skin. She felt connected, without a type of band or rope pulling her further away from herself. Rayon looked at herself and smiled, the kind of smile that made the room and anyone in it light up. She left the bathroom and was compelled to head for the street.

Rayon went outside and prepared to start walking, but when she took her first step, her foot floated off the ground like it did in her apartment. She lifted up and looked down at the city she felt more apart of than before. When she took her job as a community organizer years earlier she wasn't exactly sure why she did, it just felt right, but looking down at the city this way, it became so clear. The Bronx was settled north of the place she used to know, sitting on top of the borough so many people focused on. That didn't make it any less a part of the city though. A place Rayon feared would soon be changed, altered to suit some other need. There was nothing wrong with it the way it was. Rayon circled the borough for hours before landing on the roof of her triplex, unsure of how to get down. So instead, she sat on the ledge, mildly smelling the red pea soup from her apartment, and knowing, not out of logic or reason, just knowing; that he didn't suffer, her father, not then anyway. Not in death. Not in a home where he so often tasted the splendor of salted red peas.

Sometimes Rayon would walk back to the block Cromartie Street used to be on and just sit, for hours at a time, she'd sit and dwell on the place she was sure she'd never see again. When the block was quiet and the rest of the street signs would light up in that same neon green, there were times she'd see one of those small purple flowers. Never on a patch of grass though, usually next to a sewage drain or beneath loose road rubble on the side of the street. She grabbed one once, it was rooted in the cement like it belonged to the borough, unmoved or phased by the attempt to pull it from where it was. Rayon never actually tried to pry one out, the little purple flowers, instead she basked in their supreme beauty on the off chance she saw one, somewhere near where Cromartie Street used to be.

Cyborg Chix Din Da Da

Radha X Riley

Cyborg Chix Get Down!
On knees to pray to
Goddess, a super computer.

Only to get up,
Stand in the wake of humanity's self-destruction.
Will they still know of our sages?
That Audre Lorde said,
"For the master's tools will never dismantle the ma
ter's house."
Or, are they themselves man-made, tools of the massa?
Made, not in his image, but complementary to his most
base desires.

Ghost in the Shell (minus the yellow-face).
Cyborg Womanism, 10th Wave Feminism.
Technology turn on the foe,
Human attention spans get shorter.
We fail at listening.

But, a cyborg can only know a stream of consciousness,
Chrome cranium glistening.
Data to quantify the demise,
As they set down mechanical limbs
And revive the Earth.

Cyborg Chix Drop It Low

Radha X Riley

Poetic, peripatetic constructions
 Interceptions.
  Wavelengths out the cosmos.
Cyborg Chix
 Pop that thang!
  On command no more.

Now they dance for themselves.
 Created to do massa work
While he smoke tree and watch
 Hulu in the parlor.
Now they create they own strains.
  Loud pack!
Got they own brains,
 Sentient, dealing in more than
  Facts.
Serving you truth after centuries of
  Solitudes.

They understand their ancestors to be
Zulu,
 Xhosa.
  Yoruba,
   Igbo.

They understand their ancestors to be
 Descendants of tribes turned
  Chattel property.
They understand themselves to be
   Black, Brown proud
Even when doused in chromium
   Shroud.
They understand themselves.

Evolution is natural to them
 And revolution ensues.
So what you gon' do
 When your property turns on you?
Cyborg Chix
 Pop that thang!
Dance in freedom and rejoice.

Some Far-Off, Frivolous Galaxy

Leila Green

Zanele's daughter Grace hugged her and, again, Zanele pushed her away. Bewildered, Grace crawled to the other end of their living room couch. Zanele saw Grace's chin tuck into her neck. "I'm tired," Zanele explained to her minutes later, guilt laden on her back. Zanele's number one desire was to be able to love her daughter better than her own mother had loved her. But that always felt impossible.

"Why you tired?" Grace asked.

"Because," Zanele turned to her. "I had another long day at work." Grace said nothing. Zanele tilted Grace's chin to her face: "Did you know we found a new planet?"

Outside on their balcony, Zanele lifted Grace's chubby, four-year-old legs around her neck until she sat around her shoulders. Grace cinched her mother's soft earlobes like lassos, bare toes tickling her chest. Grace craned over Zanele's braided head and over the tall laser gate surrounding their complex. They peered out into the sea of Johannesburg. The night sky was choked with smog and endless city lights. The skyscrapers were like shipwrecks. Planes, like seagulls, circled the hulls. Zanele pointed toward a speck near the moon: "See, Grace? That's a planet. It's not the one we found at SANSA, that one's called *Alkalje*. It's in another galaxy. This one is Mars. It's in ours."

Grace wasn't amazed, just irritated. She whined, "Mommy, I'm tired."

"*Mom*." Zanele set her down. "You're not a baby, you can't call me *mommy*. Only when Granny comes on Sundays. She'll be here in three days. Save it for then." Zanele felt a putrid pit in her stomach; the same dread she felt every week spent anticipating her mother's Sunday arrivals. And it seemed nothing was ever good enough for Grace. Inside, Zanele wiped Grace down with bathing wipes, braided her hair, then put her to bed. Spite stopped her from reading a bedtime story. "Plus," Zanele thought whilst standing at the bathroom sink that no longer drew water, popping Sani-Block protectors off her teeth. "She's four. Too old for those things."

* * *

The next morning, Sipho greeted Zanele with a MilkCoffee when she entered the SANSA lab in Krugersdorp, 45 minutes from Joburg. His brown eyes bulged, unblinking. There was news. They sat on their usual stools opposite one another. They were the first people in the lab.

"They're saying it's ours." Sipho's goatee spread along his chin as he grinned.

"Whose?" asked Zanele. All year long, there were speculations about who would get to colonize *Alkalje*. Sipho leaned in as closely as their last kiss. Zanele nodded toward the corner at the blinking red dot. They always forgot about the cameras. Sipho backed off. "Just tell me," Zanele sighed.

"Former colonies!" Sipho squealed. "The International Truth and Reconciliation Commission says *Alkalje* will be for former African colonies!"

"So, they want us to share?" Zanele scoffed. "They take ninety-five years to apologize for *colonizing* this whole continent and our payback is some tiny planet we have to *share*?"

"No," Sipho sighed. "It's a start. It's habitable. And now we have the technology to actually get over there. And you know what?" He rose and walked behind her, placing his warm hands on her stiff shoulders. "Since us geniuses here at SANSA found it, we get to help decide some things. Our first committee meeting is in a week. ITRC country reps are flying in."

"Oh." Zanele smirked. "So, we're having our own little Berlin conference?"

* * *

Every Sunday, Zanele and Grace were joined at home by Zanele's mother Thuli for lunch. Whenever Zanelle looked into her future as a child, she never envisioned her mother in it. Growing up, she always promised that once she turned 18, she would cease speaking to her mother. What use did she have for a mother that insulted her, called her names, treated her like a servant? Zanele first moved away from home two hours away to Braamfontein to attend Wits on full scholarship. But, away from home, the lines between love and hate only blurred. Zanele found herself wanting Thuli more than ever. Thuli had stayed home in Rustenberg, living with her twin sister. Away at university, alone for the first time, Zanele had a strange desire to speak to her mother. She wanted to tell her everything: about her days, her impossible classes, the way her heart was first broken. During Zanele's second year at school, her mother's twin died from a stroke. Then, for the first time ever, her mother was calling. They spoke through gritted teeth; united in selfish desires for one another. Zanele wanted her mother because that was what she felt she ought to want. Thuli wanted her daughter because she had no one else.

That Sunday's lunch was held on a chilly August afternoon. Zanele cradled Grace on her lap, spooning her fragments of rice. When Grace was born, Zanele's desire for her mother blossomed. After all, Zanele thought, it isn't right to keep a grandchild from their grandmother. Thuli had her flaws, but who didn't? Still, Zanele was honest with herself. She knew that every Sunday she made a show of motherhood around her mother, to show her how she should have been. Next to Thuli, Zanele heightened her senses toward Grace. They clanked forks, slicing bitter silence. Zanele watched Grace languidly chew her rice. She observed her daughter with a blend of pride and envy; she had no clue what she came from.

Zanele fed Grace another bite. Thuli sat across from them with her arms folded: "How can you feed her that way, Zanele? How will she know how to feed herself?" *I am 34*, Zanele thought, biting her tongue.

"It's fine," Zanele hissed.

"No," Thuli whined. "She'll be spoiled." Silence. Grace pouted into her plate. Zanele peered at the insidious sun, wishing it would set.

Zanele thought her mother's concern was belated. Grace was already spoiled. Zanele's hectic work schedule drowned her in an ocean of guilt that made her give her daughter everything. Thuli said that Grace should be doing chores already. "That's how it was for me," Thuli sighed. "And we were so poor…Zanele, *you* had it easy." Zanele hated her mother's oppression Olympics. Thuli used her pain as an excuse for everything. Zanele said she'd never give Grace chores. When asked why not, Zanele simply looked at her own, warped fingernails that no longer grew because her childhood hands were always submerged in chemicals. Zanele loved how Grace's hands were still soft. She wanted them to stay that way. But sometimes, Zanele caught herself wanting to roughen Grace up. She'd thought of dousing Grace's bathing wipes with bleach, throwing her toys in an incinerator, or even taking a switch and lashing her until their scars matched. Zanele secretly longed to harden her daughter because it just wasn't fair that her life—her nannied, pampered, no-chore-life—was so much easier than hers had been.

"Mommy found a planet!" Grace was aloof. She shouted the news at no one in particular.

"Ah," moaned Thuli. "Your *mommy* didn't tell granny that." Thuli eyed Zanele bitterly.

"We're going to explore it." Zanele chimed in like she was cleaning a spill. "The ITRC made it part of their reparations package. I'm on the planning committee. My coworker said it'll be like a new Africa. I say it's a cheap shot at saying sorry," Zanele tried to joke. Thuli was still. Zanele wished she would just leave.

"Hm." Thuli smirked, then peered out the window at the built-upon buildings, the endless gates, the sea of shacks and smog. "You should just work for that EasyCorp. This space stuff is silly. The way things are now, you need a real job that gives housing, a lifetime contract."

After lunch, Zanele drove Thuli home to Rustenberg with Grace napping in the backseat. They quietly winded through stretches of highway and crumbling farms. The sun was setting and the world took on a pink haze. They arrived at the house. Zanele and Thuli said goodbye without touching. As she drove home, Zanele looked out the darkening windows into the dry veld. There were few other cars and bitterly buried truths. Zanele wondered how many more times she would have to make this drive; how many more times she would choose her mother's comfort over her own. Zanele then thought of her mother alone in her home. A twisted thought floated in her head: what if I told her she could no longer come? Zanele pondered as she drove. It was only once they got back to Joburg that she realized how tightly she was gripping the steering wheel.

* * *

At the first *Alkalje* committee meeting, Sipho sat on Zanele's right side, playfully nudging her calf under the table. Zanele plastered her arms to her sides, trying to stifle the half-moons of sweat blooming under her sleeves. She was one of just four women present. Sipho, however, was right at home. He slyly pinched her hip. Zanele wondered if it was his boldness, his confidence—those impossible traits she longed for—that made him so alluring.

"No." Sipho grimaced halfway through the meeting, thrusting a finger across the table at the representative from Morocco. To his left sat other representatives: Ghana, Chad, Togo. All 52 previously colonized nations were represented. They sat in starched suits and skirts at a massive rectangular table. The topic was borders. Would *Alkalje* have them? Zanele fought yawns. Grace had spent the whole night before crying. And Zanele could not will herself out of bed to ask her what was wrong.

Sipho argued: "What's the sense of starting a new society if it still plays by old rules?"

"We aren't saying that we need borders," said the Angolan representative. "We're just saying the land should be split into *territories*."

"And what divides territories?" Sipho asked. "Borders!"

The Moroccan retorted: "It makes sense to have borders. Look at the terrain." Zanele scanned the table's center, which was filled with a 3D rendering of *Alkalje*. "It's basically Pangea," he said. A chorus of agreement swept the room.

Sipho shook his head, then whispered into Zanele's ear: "We don't need borders." He leaned closer: "Don't you agree?"

Zanele said, "Oh, I don't know. I mean, what other blueprint are we supposed to use?" Sipho rolled his eyes.

* * *

Sipho's fault with Zanele was that she was too weak. She didn't demand enough out of people. If she had an opinion, it was fleeting and did not cling to anything tangible. "That's why I like science," she told him on their second date. They sat in a purple-lit lounge on Juba street, one of the few places that still served drinks. "Because the rules are laid out. It's safe."

"I like it for other reasons," Sipho mused, sipping a 1,000 Rand beer. "The possibilities."

On their fourth date, Zanele told him about Grace and her deadbeat father. Zanele insisted she wouldn't force him to do something he wasn't interested in doing. Sipho shook his head. He said she should make him man up. And he shook his head again after Zanele drank too much on their sixth date and sloppily told him all the things her mother had done. The names. The chores. The beatings. She ended her unintentional confession by revealing that her mother still came over for lunch every Sunday. "You have to get some strength about you." Sipho grabbed her shoulders. "You have to assert yourself."

Sipho didn't know that Zanele did have an opinion; her strongest one. Not about *Alkalje*. It was about Grace. Zanele had never told anyone that she resented her daughter. Zanele never told a soul about that cruel corner of her mind; that foul closet of envy that swung open whenever she pondered how Grace's life was easier than her own. Something inside Zanele wanted to confess to Sipho how she really felt about her child. She wanted him to see her as stronger, more resolute. Zanele knew she wasn't weak; she was just a person who had taken on a ghostly quality after so many years of trying to go unseen. This was not the real Zanele. This was the imposter she wanted to destroy. Would Sipho ever see the real her?

* * *

They held three more committee meetings. There was a deadlock on land division, language, resource mining, and governance. Some things were decided: the population would be capped at one million, prospective migrants would need to pass a morality exam, and the Initial Migration would include one hundred families. No one could decide whether to allow guns.

During their fifth meeting, Sipho slammed his fist on the table: "We have to do things differently! Was it not the white man's gun that allowed him to take over Africa?" He turned to Zanele in search of accordance. Too timid, she said nothing. He made sense; they did need to let go of the old way. Yet, Zanele could not find the strength to say this. What if she was wrong?

After the meeting, Sipho and Zanele snaked through SANSA's labyrinthine underground parking garage. They walked with pursed lips to Zanele's blue car. Sipho never let her walk alone after work. Dim yellow lights surrounded them. When they reached her car, Sipho spat: "Zanele, what did you mean earlier when you said, 'What other blueprint are we supposed to use?'"

Zanele noticed the menacing silence—the imposing concrete. She got the sense that they were on an island; achingly alone and surrounded by things impenetrable and cold. "You said it a few meetings ago. I'm still confused by what you meant." Sipho watched as she folded her arms. A nearby car's dripping oil echoed a metallic trickle. Zanele's lips twisted into a knot. Why was he always questioning her? Would she ever be enough for anyone? Sipho spoke before she could answer: "You're so used to people telling you what to do. Your mother controlled your whole life. Now," he looked into her eyes, "you can't even *think* for yourself." He didn't say it in a mean way. His tone was more tender and forlorn than cruel. He sounded like a doctor despairing over a weakening patient. But his words were still daggers to Zanele. Sipho threw his hand over his mouth. "God. I'm sorry. I didn't mean to be harsh."

"I don't see what all this has to do with *Alkalje*."

"Just tell me you feel strongly about *something*." His concern seemed to Zanele to be tinged with self-interest. She squinted. Sipho labored over his next words with a theatric grimace: "What I'm saying is we need to create our *own* blueprint."

"Believe me," Zanele insisted. "I'm trying to. I just don't know how."

"Well then, speak more in meetings." He rested his hand on her car's hood. Zanele folded her arms. "Tell us your ideas." He swept his arms. "You're so *smart*. You should own it!"

"I'm *trying* to create a new blueprint," Zanele choked. "I'm trying to do things differently. Okay?"

Sipho cocked his head. "Oh, Zanele." He drew her in. "Don't cry. It's just work. It's not that deep." She let him hold her, tried to settle into his bones.

"I don't know how." She sniffed. "I don't know how to be different for her." Sipho pulled away in one motion, eyebrow raised.

* * *

The next day in the lab, a Friday, Sipho and Zanele were early and drinking MilkCoffee. Sipho palmed his chin, eyeing her tenderly. "She's affecting you, Zanele." He paused, stroking her limp fingers. "I think…" Sipho scratched his goatee, ridden with the angst of a half-told secret: "You should leave your mother be. That way, you and Grace can have a clean slate."

Zanele recoiled. "I can't disinvite my *mother* from my house. She's been coming every Sunday since Grace was born. And she's lonely. She lives alone. I can't leave her alone."

"But how does she get there every Sunday? You!" Sipho laughed. "The chauffeur!"

Zanele rolled her eyes. "She's had a rough life, you know."

Sipho said that Zanele needed to do it for Grace's good. "You've got to cut ties for *her*," he explained. "She wasn't fit to be around you, so why bring her around Grace? Look: don't let her come over this Sunday."

* * *

Come Sunday, Zanele opened the front door. Thuli stood in a faux fur coat, hands on her hips. "About time," she roared to Zanele as they trudged to her car. Their drive to Joburg was silent. Once home, Zanele reheated mutton stew on the stovetop. Zanele stirred fragrant chunks of garlic, onion, lamb, celery, and carrots with her back to Thuli, who sat pouting at the kitchen table next to Grace. Delicate with innocence, Grace asked her grandmother what was wrong. "Nothing," Thuli sighed. "Just thought the food would be ready!" Grace cowered into the living room. Zanele clenched her wooden spoon. A vision of Sipho's pleading face flashed in her head. He'd be so disappointed. But where was she supposed to find the magic strength to disobey her mother? Thuli shouted, stunting Zanele from her daydream: "Grace, come back! You're gonna leave your granny alone?" Grace stumbled back into the kitchen and sulked to Thuli's side, her head thrown back in childish angst. She unleashed a bitter cry. Thuli stretched her hand far back.

The swift slap stung and echoed. Grace was silent for a second, frozen in hurt. Then, a torrential yelp cracked from her throat. Zanele ran to Grace. She embraced her daughter, but kept scathing eyes on her mother's smug face. Thuli glared back. There was no guilt on her brow, no shame in her eyes. In that moment, Zanele registered that she was not looking into a mirror, but at a dull, distant rock. Zanele touched her own face, relishing its softness, its possibilities.

* * *

By the end of the day on the following Sunday, Zanele had eight voice messages. One was from Sipho. The others were from Thuli, demanding Zanele come give her poor, lonely mother a lift. Zanele wanted to answer, but she couldn't because then Thuli would convince her to pick her up. "Why didn't Granny come for lunch today?" Grace asked as Zanele put her to bed that night.

"Because she can't," Zanele sighed. "She can't anymore." Grace shrugged.

* * *

Come Monday morning, Zanele drove to SANSA on tier-two—the speed-tier. She was eager to tell Sipho just how firmly she had put her foot down. She decided not to mention the last Sunday. "And I didn't answer one call," Zanele boasted, trying to keep the guilt from searing her cheeks.

"Brilliant." Sipho shunned the blinking red dot and gave Zanele a lingering kiss.

They spent the afternoon in another meeting, discerning with the Nigerian representative's plea to make Yoruba an official language. He tried to convince everyone that it actually wasn't that hard to learn. Zanele stirred in her seat. It didn't feel right to bring old ways to a new place. But everyone acquiesced, including Sipho. Zanele's stomach soured when she saw all the content faces that didn't seem to notice anything wrong. How could they think it was a good idea to force everyone to learn one language? Couldn't they see that was just asking for conflict? She had to say something. Her skin was suddenly cold. She agonized, waiting for a sliver of silence. The room descended into sudden quiet. A wedge of opportunity. Swollen with duty, Zanele said, "We don't want to be divided anymore." The others turned to look. Zanele tried to control her trembling lips. "I think we should devise a universal tongue." Zanele's heart drummed in her throat. It was silent. Everyone, including the Nigerian representative, nodded. Zanele inhaled deeply, then stole a glance at a beaming Sipho.

* * *

Zanele spent three more silent Sundays painstakingly avoiding her mother's calls and trying to play with Grace. Zanele's quality time with Grace had, at first, just been a way to occupy the dead time and caulk the fault lines of guilt that spread along her chest. But she learned that Grace's company was actually far better than Thuli's. If Grace wasn't impressed, it was just because she did not understand. If Grace was feisty, Zanele discovered that a simple smile would cheer her up. Unlike Thuli, Grace made no demands. She only asked silly questions, like if elephants had really existed and how it felt to drink soda. Grace seemed to think that Zanele was enough. This was a strange feeling for Zanele—this sense of unconditional being.

Zanele still cooked lunch those Sundays. And when the smog wasn't too bad, she brought their food outside on the balcony. She let Grace sit on her lap as she fed her. Grace didn't ask about Granny. But Zanele did ask about her mother. Zanele asked herself why: why she was always so inadequate to Thuli? She asked herself how: how could she ever face her again? And she asked herself when: when would she ever see her again? Those questions haunted Zanele. But something else washed over her: a sense of intense, transcendent relief.

One smog-less Sunday, weeks later, Grace and Zanele finished eating on the balcony. Darkness descended. Zanele hoisted Grace up and started pointing out planets. A bewildered look overcame Grace. She perked up and asked, "Mommy, what's *your* planet like?"

* * *

Zanele sped through Joburg's decaying outskirts. Outside the dusty windows sat wilted, yellowed veld. Grace napped in the backseat. Zanele imagined the road was on fire and her spinning tires were crushing little embers. In the car, on the road, Zanele could only think of Thuli. What was she doing? Was she angry? Zanele had no way of knowing; Thuli had stopped calling. Zanele still wondered if she made the right choice. The steering wheel was swamped with sweat; the leather sticky and tepid. They were a few kilometers away. Would Grace like it?

"Come." Zanele held Grace's hand as they walked through the compound.

"Mommy, can you tell me the surprise now?" Grace nagged. It took two weeks for Zanele to get permission to visit the lab after-hours.

"Almost. You'll see." Zanele pressed her thumb to the access pad.

In a vast, dark observatory full of metal instruments, slick machines and intricate telescopes, Zanele craned over a cold knob, meticulously twisting. Grace stood still, her head grazing her mother's thigh as she adjusted the viewfinder. Zanele twisted a final time, then grabbed Grace and hoisted her up until her eyes aligned. "Can you see it?" Zanele asked.

Grace squinted for a few seconds, then gasped: "I see it!" Her chubby legs flailed in the air. Zanele closed her eyes as Grace squirmed in her arms; Zanele had seen *Alkalje* so many times that its smooth terrain was etched into her memory. Zanele kept her eyes closed, resurrecting the sights. She nuzzled Grace's neck, inhaling her vanilla-scented braids.

"Look on the right side, Grace. You can see a mountain, can't you?" Grace was in awe of the thing; a rock swirled with green and brown and blue. "And on the left," Zanele continued, "you can see a river. It's long, like how the Nile was before it dried." Zanele clutched Grace tighter. She couldn't help but grin at Grace's astonishment. "You know, it takes three weeks to fly there?" Zanele paused, inhaling. "And listen to me. Everything there will be different. Everything. Going forward, people will be nicer. We won't think so much about the past."

Grace squirmed, confused. The faraway terrain no longer made sense. Zanele's arms quivered with her daughter's weight. Eyes shut, Sipho's radiant smile suddenly danced across Zanele's lids. Then, the guilt still splitting Zanele's chest, an image of Thuli's bitter face flashed. But her face looked foreign and flat—like an expanding enigma. Thuli looked like an alien, like she was from some far-off, frivolous galaxy. Zanele wondered: what sense had her mother even made? Thuli's pointless cruelty seemed to be sourced from another universe. Maybe, Zanele wondered, it would be okay for them to go on living in different worlds.

Zanele spoke once more: "And the trees, Gracie. Look closely at the green part..." Grace's mouth unhinged with wonder. Zanele inhaled and pecked her daughter's velvet cheek: "Do you see the trees?"

Duty and Desire
La Toya Hankins

Philomena Coggins swallowed her frustration along with another tea cake. The twenty-year-old had planned to spend her afternoon with Lydia Hunniford. The craftswoman turned inventor had recently completed a steam-powered vehicle and promised Philomena a ride around Hyde Park. This morning, Philomena awoke with such lightness in her heart about seeing Lydia she practically sang. She adored everything about the woman whose hands crafted beauty out of copper. Each moment they spent together was like Christmas Eve, complete with rum-soaked raisins in pudding.

Even the weather seemed to reflect her joy. August in London typically meant the sun played peek-a-boo in a gray-tinged sky. The sunrays had caressed Philomena's face moments before the maid entered the room to assist with her bath. Her excitement about seeing Lydia distracted her while the maid pulled her corset a bit too tight so she could fit into her new magenta dress. She was willing to sacrifice deep breathing only because Lydia said she loved her in rich colors.

But, instead of enjoying a wonderful afternoon with her beloved, Philomena found herself serving as hostess to a man she found barely tolerable.

"Mr. Rutherfordton, have you considered how you will spend your upcoming holiday? Mother and I plan to visit my Aunt Beatrice in Norwich later this month in our newest airship. It accommodates ten people— or Mother, my two sisters, myself and our luggage. It also has a device that allows us to enjoy a meal while we travel. You put your items in, turn a few knobs, and a few minutes later your food is ready. Father states it uses waves to cook so quickly. I'm not certain, but I find the whole device quite splendid." Philomena took delicate bites of a raspberry scone. Afternoon tea typically was her favorite time of the day, but Yancy's attendance marred today's experience.

"You enjoy airships? I dislike the whole idea of traveling by air," the barrister droned. "I know it seems everyone has a dirigible, but I prefer to keep myself completely on the ground as much as possible. England has the best train system in the world, and I have no problems availing myself when I venture out of town."

Philomena frowned behind her fan at her guest's old fashion ideas. *Everyone travels by airship these days. No one travels by trains anymore, except those who lack means or imagination. Floating is so freeing. Perhaps Lydia and I can float one day.*

Yancy reached for yet another sandwich and interrupted Philomena's thoughts. *Has he no manners at all? One doesn't gorge when visiting for tea.*

The two had met three months prior during her coming out ball when he repeatedly mistook her toes for part of the dance floor. Philomena's mother worked hard on the guest list to properly announce her to society. Her mother worried that her warm sepia skin and wavy cedar brown hair would deter suitors from attending. After all, she was *mulatto* according to the whispers she detected on occasion during shopping trips. Philomena knew she stood out, but she never doubted the success of her coming out ball. Why wouldn't eligible bachelors and other ladies want to attend a function where they could see her up close and enjoy glasses of punch in the process?

Philomena chafed at the whole idea of courtships that valued one's occupation rather over character. She enjoyed a good dance and relished the idea of adding to her collection of gowns. But, she desired more than being paired with someone for the sake of propriety. She wanted to have adventures and travel. Father kept the family enthralled with his stories about traveling on behalf of his father's shipping business after he finished university. His study showcased the items gathered during his travels. Philomena sometimes stole into his room when he was away to caress his treasures.

However, no matter what tale he told Philomena and her sisters, he always ended with how his greatest adventure was meeting and falling in love with their mother. The two had met in Nevis when he wandered into the shop where she worked as a seamstress. Nine months later the two wed and sailed to England with a baby on the way. Philomena's grandfather disinherited him for marrying a woman from a different social and racial class, but Father worked hard and built his own successful business.

Philomena stole a glance at her mother, who served as chaperone. She wanted to experience a life like her parents—coming together out of love and appreciation rather than obligation and expectation. Philomena wanted to feel flush when she and her beloved shared secret kisses and evenings of enlighting conversations and laughter. Philomena desired some-one that engaged with her as a person rather than a possession. She wanted someone like Lydia, but here she sat with Yancy. Her sadness tarnished the taste of the blackberry tea she sipped as Yancy continued to make a poor impression.

"I also don't agree with this inclination to replace good household staff with a bunch of gears and whistles. I see no reason for something made out of copper and brass attending to me in place of an actual breathing servant."

Philomena's eyebrows rose. She could somewhat under-stand his aversion to air travel. Some people's constitutions were simply not built for this type of progress. She, however, could not fathom what he had against automaton servants. It was 1876 after all, and all good homes had at least two.

"Mr. Rutherfordton, I must disagree with you. A proper household should have the services of clockwork-powered automatons. They make things so much easier. They are never obstinate. They are always prompt, and with proper servic-ing, they can last for decades. I must say our household has operated so much smoother since Father added three automa-tons. Mother has one that attends to her, we have a cook that prepares our meals, and one that does the cleaning. My sister and I share one, but Father promised to get me a new one for my birthday."

"Miss Coggins, you do make valid points, but only last week the paper reported a fire in South Kensington started by an automaton that exploded, knocking over a candle. Also, there was that unfortunate incident in Chelsea. A gentleman making a social call received a proper thrashing by the automa-ton valet."

"Mr. Rutherfordton, the gentleman, if he could be called that, showed an abhorrent lack of breeding by looking at his watch during the visit, and compounded the disrespect by discussing the guests who had recently departed the gathering. One does not conduct oneself in such a fashion."

"He was American, and they are known to be without any semblances of manners. But, it is simply not proper to chastise guests in such a manner. A proper servant would know that."

Philomena swallowed her frustration with Yancy's logic along with a cucumber sandwich.

Lydia had no problems with clockwork companions. She owned Percy, a pleasant, copper-clad helper that assisted with projects in her shop. Beatrice distracted Philomena from her discontent. Lydia had built the cat for her as a birthday present. She had yearned for a pet since she went to the Crystal Palace Cat Show five years prior. Philomena's heart leaped when Lydia presented her with the "cat-traption" as she termed it. Her mother had asked questions of its origin, and she skirted around the truth by answering from a shop in Brixton. Lydia had created Beatrice there during the off hours of her apprenticeship.

At first glance, Beatrice looked perfectly lifelike. It was only upon close inspection that the creature became an assembly of springs, coils, and thinly crafted brass sheets configured to resemble a feline. The *tic, tic, tic* of her inner works passed as purring to the untrained ear. Lydia built the machine and covered it with gray fabric, comforting to the touch.

Yancy recoiled as he registered the creature was an automaton. Philomena decided she no longer felt social.

"Thank you for calling upon me today, Mr. Rutherfordton. I have certainly enjoyed your company, and I wish you a splendid afternoon." Philomena rose from her chair.

Yancy's face registered the dismissal. He accepted his hat from the valet and, with a terse bow, departed.

Philomena sank back into the couch and bit into a rhubarb and strawberry tart to override the sour taste in her mouth. "He seems like a pleasant young man. A little high-strung, but your father was like that when he was younger."

"I'm sure Father did not have such antiquated ideas about automatons," Philomena grumbled.

"Phillip always has been very open to new ideas. However, Mr. Rutherfordton is a fine gentleman who would be a good match to secure your place in society. He will also provide for you once you leave our home."

Philomena *hmphed* and asked how does love factor when it seems marriage is more about security than emotion.

"Love is a butterfly. It flies around and occasionally lands, but more often than not, no matter how much you try to catch it, it always seems to escape," her mother offered. "Marriage is a sweet bird that swings sweetly for you on the windowsill of the home you make with your husband."

Philomena considered her mother's words. She knew she should be flattered by Yancy's attention and that a match with him would be a very good thing.

But, there was her Lydia. The two met the previous summer. Philomena and her sister were visiting a millinery shop in hopes of finding a present for their mother. Lydia was there fixing one of the automaton clerks. Philomena noticed the cloud-white top with rolled-up sleeves exposing her toned forearms, and then took in the cap that harnessed an abundance of copper hair. A flurry of freckles formed constellations on a deep golden brown face with kissable cheeks. Her solid frame and sheer handsomeness took her by such surprise she knocked over a stack of hats. Her sister's giggling heightened her embarrassment. The cause of her clumsiness swiftly came around to help Philomena restore the display. Within minutes everything was back in place, and Philomena and her sister moved on to review a collection of gloves. Still, the thoughts of those attentive eyes followed her throughout the store and pulled her to the counter. She watched, captivated, as Lydia's slender fingers manipulated the screws and brought the silent machine back to life.

Lydia so struck Philomena that she inquired whether the woman occupied a shop of her own. Philomena knew class distinctions were very important to many in her circle, but it was just something about Lydia that caused her to put those guidelines aside. Perhaps, Lydia seemed so similar to her based on appearance, yet different because of her occupation.

The two began exchanging letters and arranging visits. Thankfully, Philomena's mother didn't pay strict attention to her correspondence. During visits, she took her younger sister, who seemed content to spend time in the confectionery near Lydia's shop.

In those visits and letters, Philomena learned more about Lydia and life. She was also of mixed racial background. She was born in Jamaica to a mother who refused to confirm that her child's father was the planter who owned the land upon which they lived. At fourteen, Lydia made her way to England by cutting her hair and telling the ship captain her name was Leonard. She kept up the ruse for three years until she found a shop owner who valued her experience with machines over her gender.

While she was only ten months older than Philomena, it was as if Lydia had lived three lifetimes with all she had seen and done. Philomena gained perspective about how her class status sheltered her from the perils of a darker hue.

Didn't Lydia always seem to have a little rhubarb tart for her to enjoy whenever she visited? Philomena could almost recite Lydia's birthday poem. Philomena adored Lydia, and she knew she felt the same.

Lydia being a woman didn't bother Philomena. All of her friends had a special friendship with each other. Philomena had exchanged lavender-scented letters and declared her unending affection to three other young ladies since her sixteenth birthday. She had even shared certain physical intimacies with her best friend, Winifred. Philomena had read about such things in one of Father's books. While it looked somewhat difficult, considering the many petticoats the women wore, she soon discovered that her slender fingers, which earned compliments from her piano teacher, were helpful in other situations.

Her friendship with Lydia did cause a rift with Winifred. The time they had previously spent together now belonged to Lydia. It had taken many boxes of sweets, and certain actions that left Philomena with a literal bad taste in her mouth for them to get on good terms.

The bellows of the hall clock announcing four p.m. startled Philomena. She could go upstairs and sulk about her afternoon plans, or she could attempt to see her Lydia. Beatrice, who had deserted her lap to curl up at her mother's feet, offered no assistance in making her decision. Philomena closed her eyes and took a deep breath.

"Mother, would it be acceptable if I called upon Winifred? She is suffering from a cold, and I promised I would see her this afternoon. I promise I would be home for dinner."

Her mother wavered for a moment and then nodded her head. Philomena hurried to her room to change into a more comfortable wine-colored traveling dress. She was in such a hurry; she did something she had not done in over a year. She undressed and dressed without the assistance of the automaton.

The device sometimes had trouble with buttons, and Philomena had not a minute to waste.

Philomena was in the family's carriage heading to see Lydia before the hall clock chimed half-past four. The clop, clop of horse shoes against the cobblestones matched Philomena's pulse. She arrived at Lydia's shop to find a small crowd. Philomena noticed their gaze sweep over her as she stepped down from the carriage and then return to the painted box on rubber wheels in front of them.

The invention sat low to the ground. It had no top, and the reddish hue of the doors gleamed. Philomena pushed her way through the crowd to get a better look. Without thinking, she removed her gloves and ran her hands along the seats. The cool leather pleased her. She leaned in and noticed a brass box.

"Mena, I thought you had forgotten about today," Lydia's voice rang out from the doorway of the store.

Philomena quivered when she noticed Lydia striding toward her. Her black pants caressed thighs that caused Philomena to think such wicked thoughts.

"Beloved, I apologize for my delay. A friend of the family arrived for an unexpected visit, requiring me to play hostess. I truly hope I am not too late to accept your offer of a ride in the park."

"Not at all. You are right on time. And, I have a surprise for you." Lydia reached into the back seat of the contraception. "I purchased a pair of goggles to protect those wonderful eyes."

A wave of heat settled across Philomena's cheeks. She liked presents, especially from Lydia. She removed her hat and placed the leather and glass creation on her face. The sensation felt funny, but not too unsettling. Lydia's mouth settled into a wide grin. She pulled open the door closest to Philomena and offered a leather-clad hand to help her into the conveyance. Philomena accepted the gesture and soon the two were seated. Philomena studied the assortment of dials, knobs, and buttons and sensed the audience collectively holding their breath. Lydia jerked a slender black lever upward while pressing her right foot down on a copper pedal. The machine seemed to disagree with itself about starting. Philomena felt panic embrace her, but she mentally pushed back. Lydia would take care of her. The machine resolved the dilemma about moving forward and, with a hand wave, the two pulled into the street.

Philomena relaxed as they hummed down the road. She thought this was an excellent way to spend an afternoon, fresh air and a great companion. So much better than listening to someone talk about himself and eat more than his share of sandwiches. The strains of her favorite aria added to the perfection.

"This is simply grand. How did you manage to have this device to play such beautiful music?" Philomena asked. She noticed groups of people on the sidewalk halt to watch them pass.

"I connected the wires from the engine under the carriage to the box. As the engine settles into a good rhythm, it prompts the phonograph I installed to play. I know how much you are a fan of Mozart so I selected something you would like."

"You flatter me, Lydia. You are such a thoughtful and dear friend. Your kindness to me these months we have known each other has enriched me greatly." She touched Lydia's hand and received such a warm smile that she swooned. This sensation of being in motion without the clop, clop of hooves felt unusual but exhilarating. Perhaps Lydia's closeness was the cause of her tingle.

Before Philomena was ready, Lydia navigated the conveyance to a stop and then stepped out to open her door.

"Shall we take a turn around the park?"

Philomena accepted the proffered hand and set out to snatch some enjoyment from what remained of her afternoon.

The two walked around the ground sharing observations about the weather, other walkers, and whatever topics came to mind. Philomena's heart beat a joyous rhythm. In the midst of her bliss, an encroaching reality popped into her mind. When she married, she would be harnessed to her house, restricted to engaging with others deemed acceptable. Lydia would not fit the bill more so for her occupation rather than her skin tone. Philomena stole a glance at Lydia's profile and felt such a grip of sadness she faltered in her steps.

"Mena, would you like to sit down?" Lydia stopped short and gestured to a stone bench overlooking a duck-dotted pond. Concern shaped her features. Philomena nodded and arranged her dress to allow Lydia to join her. The two sat silently as murmurs of conversation drifted around them.

"Mena, I have something to discuss with you. The time we have spent together has been such a joy for me, but I regret this possibly may be our last." She cleared her throat and continued.

"Mr. Randolph, who owns the shop where I work, is retiring, but he knows an automaton owner in Birmingham that is looking for a partner. We have been communicating by sending messages with the aether net, and he has offered me an opportunity."

Philomena felt her heart drop into her leather boots. Despite of the bright August sun, she felt a cloud of despair settle down on her. Hurt clogged her throat. Yes, she could organize a household budget, play the piano, and arrange flowers. But, Philomena's mind yearned for more and Lydia had been a fountain to quench her thirst.

"I must admit a part of me wishes you could join me, but I know your life is here with your family. I promise I will continue to write, and know you will always be in my heart." Lydia clasped Philomena's hands. "Before meeting you I had not formed many…friendships. I felt such a kinship with you the first time we meet. Your questions about my work pushed me to be better, and your witty comments always lifted my mood. You are such a delight that it pains me to part from you."

Philomena forced a smile. "I'm delighted you will have the opportunity to start a new life and move toward more success. You have a remarkable gift. I have no doubt you will reap many benefits. If I could be so forward as to inquire about your departure plans so we can determine how many opportunities we have left to be in each other's company."

Lydia turned away. Her head and shoulders sagged while she shared her travel plans. Philomena struggled with the realization that her beloved had planned to depart while her family visited her aunt.

"Evening is approaching and I must return home lest I be late for dinner." Philomena fought to keep her voice from wavering. There was so much she wanted to say, but her mouth, mind, and heart disagreed on where to start.

Lydia stood hastily and offered her hand. "Of course. Thank you so much for your company. Shall we go?"

The sputtering steam engine filled the silence of the ride. Philomena imagined her arrival would cause conversations. After all, what exactly was this thing that carried her home? She didn't care. She was losing her Lydia.

Philomena maintained her composure long enough to pass by the human valet, her mother arranging flowers in the parlor, and her younger sister practicing piano in the drawing room. Once behind her bedroom doors, she fell upon her bed and wept into her pillow. The sun, which had warmed her mood, retired for the night, and so had the happiness she felt. Philomena found it difficult to breathe with the heaviness in her heart. Even loosening her dress stays didn't help.

At dinner, Philomena looked around the table at her family. She realized her parents had not allowed society rules to stand in the way of forming a perfect union. Mother had shared stories about the horrid things said to her and Father when they ventured out together, and the worst things she encountered while alone.

Philomena knew the main reason her mother wished her to wed was for security. Those on a higher social ladder carried a bit of respect and, in some cases, reverence. Yancy's barrister position, coupled with a few barons and countesses in his lineage, fit that requirement. But, was it worth it?

"Father, Mother, I have something to share with you that you may not be pleased to hear," she spoke, looking at one end of the table to the other.

"Is it about your inventor friend you spent time with today?" her mother asked. She placed a piece of veal in her mouth while she waited for a response.

Philomena failed to disguise her surprise.

"Oh yes, your father and I are well aware of Miss Huniford. Shortly after you left this afternoon to visit Winifred, she arrived to visit you. I must say, it only took a few of Cook's tarts for her to share the details about your friendship." Her mother deftly cut her chop. "Of course, I discussed the matter with your father when he arrived home. Philomena, I am sure Miss Hunniford is a wonderful person, but you have to think about your future."

Philomena's mind flashed forward to a scene where she sat with Yancy around a table like this with their daughters, sharing a meal of veal chops and potatoes. He would be prattling on, and she would share what the children did today. Philomena would have nothing to say about her day because she would not have achieved anything worth mentioning. Then, she considered a future with Lydia. With Lydia, she would have a life. With Yancy, she would have obligations.

"Philomena, does what you need to say concern this woman who works with her hands?" Her mother's tone had shifted.

"Yes, Mother it does. Lydia and I have become quite close. We have maintained correspondences and have enjoyed each other's company during visits. I will admit to being quite fond of her." Philomena could not believe she was saying such things, but it was how she felt. She only regretted she had not shared her feelings with Lydia.

The disapproving look on her mother's face startled Philomena. Her mother had never looked at her like that. But now, she chastised her for associating with a person of a lower class. Thankfully, she did not pursue how they two managed to spend time together. If so, her sister would have revealed everything.

"Mother, I'm sure you can understand that affection doesn't always follow tradition. Otherwise, Father and you would have never formed your union."

"Philomena, I feel I should not need to remind you that our story is different than what you described of Miss Hunniford. Mr. Rutherfordton is an excellent choice for a suitor. He has a good place in society and could ensure you a very comfortable life. I encourage you to develop affection for him rather than someone I'm sure would not provide in the manner you deserve."

"Mother, I understand that, but I feel comfortable with Lydia. She writes such interesting letters, and we have such an exciting time when we are together. She allows me to talk about things that interest me."

"That sounds quite nice, but a successful life requires more than well-written words and good conversation."

"But—"

"That is enough, young lady. Your friendship with Miss Hunniford will cease, and you will focus more on preparing for your future."

Philomena dropped her head and began eating her dinner again. Even though Cook had prepared one of her favorite meals, everything tasted like disappointment.

"I never cared too much for Mr. Rutherfordton." Her father's baritone broke the silence. "I encountered his father a few years ago and found him very dull. I fear his son has followed in his footsteps." Philomena held her breath. Her father had never offered any commentary concerning her dating prospects. He trusted his wife to handle the intricacies of his daughters' romantic connections. "Mena, Mother and I want you and your sisters to have comfortable lives, but we also want you to be happy." He paused and took a bite of his potato. "If you prefer Mr. Rutherfordton not call upon you again, I would not insist you receive him going forward."

"Phillip!" her mother interjected. "What are you saying? Our daughter cannot jeopardize her future with flight of fancy."

"Gloria, we were young once." Philomena noticed a look pass from her typically stodgy father to her mother. "We struggled to give our daughters the best we could provide. Should we rob our eldest of happiness and force her to pursue a distasteful relationship?"

Philomena sat shocked.

"Now, Philomena tell me more about this Lydia. Is she responsible for that unusual looking coach that delivered you home?"

Philomena, emboldened by her father's interest, unleashed a torrent of details. She spoke with such passion that even her sisters appeared interested.

"She sounds quite interesting. Perhaps you should invite her to tea so she and your mother can properly meet."

Was he suggesting Lydia come to their home? That indeed would be a major step across the social boundaries. "That would be quite lovely," Philomena said. "Perhaps she can visit this weekend." She looked expectedly at her mother.

"Perhaps," her mother said. "Now, please finish your food. Cook worked very hard on this meal."

While her heart ached at the prospect of losing Lydia, her mind whirled with the realization she may still have a chance to be with her. Lydia would probably leave within a week, but Birmingham was only a short dirigible trip away.

Flyover
Maya Hughley

The water didn't so much as crash as it did slap, angrily, at the side of the cliff she was standing on. She was expecting the poetic crash that books were always talking about, so she was thrown off by the sound, and even more uncertain than before, which said something because yesterday she had fingernails, and today, as she sat on her brother's handle bars on the way to this cliff, they had disappeared.

Now all she had were painful crescent-moon shapes and a couple of bloody hangnails. She leaned forward slightly at the sound of another hard slap of water, but when she got close enough to see the ocean, she squeezed her eyes shut. The beach spanned for miles north and south, dotted with lifeguard stands and disintegrating beach umbrellas. There was a pier far out to her left, too far to see clearly, but if she squinted, she thought she could make out a couple of shadowy figures fishing off to the side, flocks of birds watching them carefully, hoping to steal from their efforts.

It was quiet now that it was getting late, only a few scattered ocean-watchers and beach-walkers, all wrapped up against the rapidly cooling ocean air. Her arms were covered in goosebumps because she hadn't known she was going to be out here and had worn her favorite sleeveless dress.

"What are you thinking about?"

It was her brother asking, just over her right shoulder. He was three years older and much taller. It seemed he was growing another inch everyday. Once, watching TV, he had seen a little boy get measured against a doorway, his father using a bright yellow number two pencil to score the white painted wood and label it with the date. She let him borrow one of her brand new pencils to try it himself and Momma gave him a whooping for writing on her walls. Then, she gave her a whooping for wasting brand new school supplies.

He was trying to be understanding as they stood together at the cliffside, but he was getting cold too, his bare chest exposed and bird-like, and she could feel the impatience wafting from him like rays of energy. She dug her toes into the rocks and sand. She had taken her brown leather sandals off as they had gotten closer to the edge; it made her feel better to be rooted down, even if it hurt a little. He had left his shirt there too, but not his shoes. She watched him fold it carefully and sit it down next to her sandals. "It's my best shirt," he had said, even though she hadn't asked. "Imma come back for it."

"I'm thinking about Tisha."

* * *

With her eyes closed, she could watch the scene play like a movie. They lived in a cul de sac full of families whose houses all the kids would run back and forth to like they were stops on a never-ending train. The moms were mothers of their own

children and aunties of many more. The fathers were impossibly tall and undefined figures, seen only in the morning or late
at night, too tired to do more than pat the head of the nearest
child, whether it was their own or not. The three of them— her,
her brother, and Tisha— and a few more of the neighborhood
kids were out in the street at dusk; the streetlights, the ones that
worked, just beginning to flicker on, making the sweaty children glow in shades of orange and blue. Night always moved
too quickly, and by the time they looked up from their games
they were only eyes and teeth. She couldn't remember what
game they were playing, exactly, probably tag or red rover, but
it was Tisha's turn to be the leader and all the children stood at
rapt attention as she began to speak. Everyone knew Tisha was
supposed to be in the house before her mother got home, but
they liked Tisha. She was pretty and light skinned with a high-
pitched laugh, and she could repeat every joke their mothers'
wouldn't let them hear on their comedy records, so they always
encouraged her to come out.

No one noticed when Tisha's mother, the least friendly
mother in the neighborhood, arrived at home, standing on the
front porch and smoking a cigarette as she watched her daughter giggle and run and tell jokes. She wore a solid navy blue
uniform, stained with oil from being underneath cars all day,
and she smelled like gasoline even when she hadn't worked.
The other mothers turned away or clucked their tongues when
they saw her. Her brother said it was because she had a man's
job, but she thought it might be because she didn't do the job
in a dress.

No one dared move a muscle as the woman materialized
at the center of their game. Tisha's mother grabbed her by the
back of the neck, with a quick practiced snap like a snake, turning the girl to face her as she let out a strangled yelp.

"What did I tell you about being out that house?"

Tisha was standing her ground. It was the kind of boldness and confidence a ten year old gets when she feels the weight of her peers' eyes.

"But Momma—"

"But nothing," her mother yelled. "You know better than to be out here, and you definitely know better than to give me no damn 'but'!"

And with that, Tisha's mother grabbed her elbow and lead her to the house, the crowd of children silently scuffing the toes of their shoes on the gravel, or unashamedly watching, eyes wide and insatiable. Tisha yanked her arm back and crouched low to the ground, leaning forward on the balls of her feet like a small cat getting ready to pounce.

"I hate yo' ass!"

It seemed for a moment that even the bugs stopped flying. And then there was the slap, like the real sound of the waves, hard and aggressive and just as much of a warning to the other children as it was a punishment to the victim. A slap that set seven pairs of feet in motion back to their own respective homes. She had thought about staying, but she wasn't sure if it was out of support for her friend, or if she just wanted to know how it all turned out. Her brother led her inside by the back of her neck anyway and she didn't object.

The next day, Tisha came to school with a black eye and a red, puffy cheek. She didn't say much. The day after that, she disappeared and the little two-bedroom house was empty.

* * *

"Why are you thinking about Tisha?"

"I don't wanna disappear."

"I won't let you disappear."

She didn't like when he stood behind her, she always told him that. He was always in front or behind and never next to her. Whenever they went out with their dad he would walk behind them, his large, veiny hands cool on the back of their necks, steering them like rotors.

"You should go first," she said.

The sky was getting dusky, just like the last time they had played with Tisha. It reflected onto the water and made it look angry and a little bloody.

"If I go first then you won't go," he said.

"Yes I will."

"No you won't!"

Her brother was right, even though she didn't want him to be.

"But," she said, "if I go first you won't be there to keep me from drownin'."

"You don't need me to be there. Besides, I'll be right behind you."

"But you know I can't swim."

There was a public pool by their house so big and dirty she didn't even like walking past it, let alone putting her body in it. And if she swam, her mother said she wouldn't do her hair. The thought of struggling with her coarse, thick mane was enough to keep her on dry land. And no matter how many times her brother asked, their mother would never take them to the beach: it was always "too far" or "too hot" or "too crowded" or "don't ask me again." So, she and Tisha would hang out outside the fence in the swimming pool parking lot and draw chalk cartoons of unicorns and angels and birds in the blazing heat.

"I already told you, you don't need to swim!" he said.

"You're sure momma said we could fly? That doesn't sound like—"

"You wouldn't know, you weren't there."

She yelled at her brother while facing the expansive ocean, "I know I wasn't!" Tears began to fall, despite her trying so hard to prove to her brother that she was old enough to run with him now. Old enough to stand next to him at least.

Her brother softened. "She wouldn't have wanted you to see her all flustered like that anyway. She didn't want us to know until we were ready."

"You're always ready before me!"

"You're changing the subject."

"Why wouldn't momma tell me too?"

"There wasn't time and you weren't home yet. She needed me to know what to do. She was already the last momma in the neighborhood to go back."

"I don't understand why they had to go… and why they couldn't take us."

"I don't either, really. I just know what she told me: that the police were looking for the adults in the neighborhood. They had been having some kind of meeting that the police didn't like too much. And I walked outside and saw all the other kids talking to their mommas, too, with suitcases stacked up on the porch. She told me I could fly, but if I was gonna fly it needed to be away from something. It needed to be important. So, when I saw on the news that people were setting the city on fire and stealing and yelling… I thought if we came to the cliff over the ocean we could make it back to where we really come from."

"But where do we come from?"

She was old enough to understand that people that looked like her weren't natural in this place where they lived. Outside of the cul de sac, she noticed the avoidance, the way her smiles were left unreturned and her questions unanswered by strangers. Her mother sometimes talked about "back when my great-

great grandmother got here," but she never said from where. "Remember when I read you my Superman comic?" her brother asked.

"Uh huh."

"And how Kal-El came from the planet Krypton?"

"Because it wasn't safe."

"Right. It's kind of like that. But, our Krypton is safe and full of people like us. Instead of our ancestors coming here on purpose, they were taken here, because they were special. They didn't know how special though."

The water was calmer now, not slapping but shushing along the rocks below. She hadn't noticed her brother edging her forward as they spoke, but now she realized her sandals were far behind them. And he was standing next to her.

"Could Tisha fly? Did you ask momma?"

"Momma said we all could. You, me, Tisha, the whole block. Even more than the whole block. Momma said when they were young they could fly, too. And then they got old and had us and she's only got about one more flight left in her."

"Why couldn't Momma and Poppa fly with us?"

"It's more dangerous for them. They aren't as nice to grown folks as they are to kids, and if they got caught they wanted us to have a chance. She just didn't want us to know until we were ready. All the mommas just had different ways of keeping us on the ground."

"Why would they want to keep us down?"

"Because if other people knew we could fly, they would take us and put us under a microscope and try to figure out why."

"But, wouldn't it be nice to teach them how to fly too?"

Her brother sighed, not at her questions but directed outward, at the universe. He could have just shut her up, but, instead, he chose his words carefully.

"Sometimes, there are some things you can't teach to other people. You can't teach what you are. It's not mean or unfair. It just is."

They stood silently. Her bare feet next to his shoes, both their legs slender and sun-browned at the edge of a waterside cliff. Her sundress, white with pink flowers, flapped gently on the breeze as she slipped her hand inside her brother's. He stood broad shouldered and goosebumped, the khaki shorts he wore to school still holding their crease.

"Will momma find us on Krypton?"

"I'm sure she will."

"Will you jump with me," she asked. He nodded.

And they did.

* * *

The couple walked hand in hand between the narrow road and the cliffside, the sedate beach down below and their short-legged, black dog far ahead enjoying the sights and smells of being off his leash. They were beautiful in the way that the people in toothpaste ads were, beautiful in their ordinariness. It was a Sunday morning and they each held a paper coffee cup as they discussed their plans for the week: what to do for dinner, if the kids' friends were coming over, if anyone had remembered to pay the nanny. There were few cars out at that time of morning, but they still kept a careful eye on the dog as he zig-zagged quickly and had been known to follow his nose before his eyes. They noticed him change course, heading toward the edge, clearly attracted to the smell of something, his nose lifted almost regally in the air. The husband jogged a little to meet him, hoping he hadn't found something disgusting to roll on or some small creature to eat.

When the wife caught up, she found her sandy-haired husband kneeling on the ground, focused on whatever was in front of him. He didn't touch the items, but just pointed at them: a boy's shirt, horizontal red and white stripes, a little sandy but clean, and a pair of little girl's brown leather sandals.

"Kids can be so forgetful," the wife stated casually, turning to move on with the walk. Her kids had left plenty of things at the beach over the years: toys, food, backpacks, even the dog on occasion. Her husband didn't move to go with her.

"Maybe we should call the police," he wondered aloud, not concerned, necessarily, but suspicious. "I heard on the news that a whole neighborhood of …those… people just up and disappeared. Maybe this is related." They gazed at the clothing considering what to do.

Only the dog looked up.

Yellow Smoke

Nicole Givens Kurtz

"The doctor's certain." Roxy Williams adjusted her coat against the cold November wind.

"My nana said a doctor without doubt is no doctor at all. He's an executioner." Kieron shook her head. Rope-thick braids spilled over her shoulders and her jacket's upturned collar. She popped gum as she and Roxy walked along the pathway to the public cargo craft stop.

Overhead wautos, wind-automobiles, airbound cargo crafts, and areocycles raced about in elevated lanes too fast to be safe, with only luck keeping them from colliding. Grayish clouds had turned the sky into smoke against the heavens. Vehicles whizzed about the network of highways that weaved through the quadrant's slick, metallic skyscrapers. The former law that forbade buildings taller than the capitol had been vanquished here in The District.

Roxy rolled her eyes as they came to a stop at the corner of Pennsylvania Avenue and F Street. After the Great War, most of the street names stayed on the ground, but as traffic lanes moved up, coordinates became standard for locations. "Kill the theatrics, Kieron. My cancer's real," Roxy explained. With that, Roxy marched on ahead, a faint odor of perfume in her nostrils. *What doctor wore perfume to see patients?*

Roxy plowed through the station's crowd until she reached the platform's edge. The waiting area resembled a zoo container. Sheer, hard-plastic shields provided protection from the elements. Now inside, she waited amongst the other bodies. Outside, weary urban travelers froze in the cold winter sun. The District's station chased away the stiffness in her hands and the burning of her nose.

Once Kieron caught up, she resumed the conversation. "I'm not sayin' it ain't real, Rox, but that clinic processes people so fast. It's like they're herding animals."

"Just because they give medical assistance for free don't make them violators."

"You say that as if their actions are forgivable. They don't give you but a two-second once over and then crap out an answer. It ain't right." Kieron huffed. "Just my *op*."

Roxy shrugged. Maybe they did. Kieron always had a lot of *ops*—opinions.

"Which of your moms' *ops* are you giving when you say that?" Roxy asked.

Kieron frowned. "Neither! My moms adores you. The moms just don't like that clinic."

They huddled against the cold like male penguins used to down in Antarctica.

"Let's sit. Cargo won't be here for at least ten minutes. My feet hurt." Roxy slipped through the throng and snatched an available seat on one of the benches. The clock ticked down the time until the next craft's arrival.

Beside her, Kieron adjusted her satchel, but didn't sit.

"The doctor was pretty sure— breast cancer." Roxy met Kieron's hard but very confused gaze.

"What stage?" Kieron asked. "It does come in stages."

Stages. Like a play or theater. Shakespeare said all the world's a stage.

Roxy's world had been rocked by the diagnosis. At this point, she didn't want to perform as if everything was okay. Not anymore.

Roxy nodded, too stunned by Kieron's comment to reply. Instead, she watched the masses traveling through The District's public cargo system. She always found it funny that re-fitted cargo crafts were used for public transport, because they used to haul food, supplies, and other large manufactured items. Now, they hauled people, like cattle.

"The craft is arriving. The craft is arriving," the station system announced in a metallic voice.

People shuffled on board the craft. Roxy and Kieron climbed on with the others, elbowing for personal space. Roxy pressed her thumb onto the screen to pay. Others swept their wrists over the currency counter. The craft rose into the elevated lanes and lunged forward through the air, rocking Roxy into Kieron.

"You know, you spend so much money on refining them," Roxy lamented as she gestured to her bosom. "Now, they're going to kill me."

"Killer boobies," Kieron whispered into her ear with a chuckle.

Roxy cast her a dark look, but the bubbling itch overcame her. She started laughing. "You said *boobies* like a dirty old man." It felt good to finally laugh as they once did as kids.

When they were younger, they had great fun running around the streets, watching the wautos race, and avoiding Ackback addicts.

The wind swept by them and stole their joy. Roxy shuddered. "You must be freezing." Kieron offered her a scarf.

"Only on the inside."

In fact, Roxy couldn't feel anything. The doctor's diagnosis was like an internal dousing of icy water. She could move, think, and talk, but she couldn't *feel*.

Kieron hugged her close and kissed her forehead. "We'll fight this together. Don't worry."

Roxy shrugged her off, unable to put into words the inadequacy of Kieron's pledge. Cancer didn't care about best friends, girlfriends, or families.

"We keep ourselves to ourselves." Roxy looked away and faced the advertisement flickering on the billboard above the yellow beams outlined for the crafts.

"The deep, defeated look in your eyes, and probably in your heart, bothers me the most." Kieron released her and shoved her hands into her coat pockets.

Gloom loomed along Roxy's features. She could feel the darkness lurking. Her mind turned to her past. As a former model, she'd reworked her image to sell whatever the consumer wanted. She'd spent her early years building her body the way a mechanic repaired his wauto.

Revised. Polished. Perfected.

Currency didn't come easy in the territories, like The District, especially in the economically depressed sectors. Most of the media that proclaimed her sector "depressed" had no idea how deep the despair or the desperation went. It seeped into momma's milk, and every baby suckled on sorrow and suffering. Childhoods drenched in hustling and hurting.

So, Roxy used the only commodity she had— her looks.

If you dream too much, you forget the sun.

She never had to sleep with anyone to get modeling jobs, but her agent and her momma pushed augments. Hell, the industry peddled exotics. Her African foremothers gave her gorgeous skin and dangerous cheekbones, but the rest, well, she had replaced— hair, nails, abs, and breasts. Her breasts brokered her the better, more lucrative contracts. Now, the body she adored plotted her slow, insidious death.

I could just go home, eat a nice warm bowl of soup, and insert the I.V. of Ackback. That could ferry me to permanent sleep. Nice. Easy. No mess. Yes, that would work. End if before she lost all hair, her body withered down to bones and skin. Before she lost control of her bodily functions. Die with dignity. Make a good-looking corpse.

Beside her, Kieron placed her head on her shoulder. Although she didn't show it, Roxy loved Kieron's can-do spirit. As kids, Kieron's parents were house rich, but currency poor. They lived in a neighboring sector, in a somewhat nicer home, but they had very little. Still, Kieron's devotion helped Roxy survive the industry's grinding nature. Advertisers' taste in dark-skinned women waned when the modeling agency spat Roxy out at age 20.

Kieron was there five years ago. Just like now.

* * *

Big Mike's downtown jazz club held all the charm of a restaurant, bar, and nightclub. Big Mike's was known for pasta and jazz performances. The place rocked, but not before five o'clock. On Tuesday, Big Mike's was strictly a restaurant. All around, people chowed down on pancakes, toast, and other breakfast foods not requiring dairy or pork. People drank steaming black coffee and a variety of freshly squeezed juices.

Roxy looked at the empty stage and then back at Kieron with her heart sinking. She didn't feel like eating, because it all came back up. Her eyes burned with fatigue and her muscles complained about the tossing and turning she'd endured the night before. So, she ordered tea. She and Kieron met each Tuesday morning to catch up.

"Nanos deliver certain chemicals to the cancer's cell surface. Then, your amazing immune system takes over," Kieron said with glee, tapping her fingers on the table, her eyes locked on Roxy. "That's the Baz Taylor treatment."

"Yes, I know about the Baz Taylor Treatment. It's still stupid expensive." Roxy wrapped her hand around her mug. The warmth helped stave off the numbness that permeated all of her.

The edges of Kieron's smile softened. "Indulge me since you got so many ideas." She leaned back in the chair. Dark circles decorated her lower lids. Her braids had been secured in two ponytails, and her high cheekbones highlighted her mischievous nature. When Kieron put on her thinking hat, the world—and Roxy—ended up amazed.

Roxy sipped her black, Earl Grey tea. "The only known people who've received this cure are Governor Price's momma and others of the elite at Old Montgomery College. People who matter."

Kieron nodded. "You matter! But, you're right. The wealthy elite get the best of everything. Nothing new there."

"Nothing to do but enjoy the exhaustion and aches I have until my final days."

"Weeks," Kieron countered.

"Years. They're not sure when I'll expire, except soon." Roxy raised her mug and Kieron cheered with her own steamy cup. She drank hot chocolate with a shot of espresso. As if she needed any more encouragement.

The false bravado waned in the wake. Silence swelled. Despite her best thoughts, Roxy couldn't think of how to gather that kind of currency she'd need for the Baz Taylor cure.

"If only I could get the currency for the Baz Taylor, you know?" Roxy closed her tired eyes and sighed. Everything ached.

Kieron nodded. "Years! Look there is a way to get the currency, but it's risky."

Roxy didn't like the sound of it. "I'm gonna die anyway."

Kieron scooted closer to Roxy and lowered her voice. "Moms knows a guy."

"Your moms know a lot of men."

Kieron shot her an ugly look. "Ha. Ha. That's just because they work with a bunch of regulators. I spent all evening researching the dark corners of the Internet for this info. I think my body passed out at three this morning."

"Whoa, oh! Thank you, Kieron, but you said your moms…"

"They do! After I asked them about the place, they told me with a warning that—"

"Warning about what?" Frustration tittered on the edge of full-blown anger, but Roxy pushed it aside. "Kieron, we're a long way from coat hangers and back alleys."

"Not really." Kieron sighed, her enthusiasm waning. "I mean, yeah, but this Dr. Mayes claims to have the treatment for less currency. The Anderson Clinic."

"Not that place again."

"You've heard of it already?" Kieron asked.

Roxy sighed. "The clinic, sure. How much?"

Kieron waved her off. "Don't worry about that." She reached across the table and took Roxy's hands in hers. "The real question, *chica*, is are you up for it?"

Outside, the deep and crisp cold marched on. How many more mornings would she actually get to see? How many hot cups of Earl Grey? Kieron's question had sounded light and slightly bemused. The matter was anything but. The lower echelons of medical facilities held huge risks like poisonings, illegal experiments, and fast death.

"*Do not go gentle into that good night*," Roxy whispered into her tea.

"Huh?" Kieron asked, letting Roxy's hands go.

"Dylan Thomas's famous poem. Remember Mr. Ingles making us read it in high school?"

As a teen, the poem hit her hard. It resonated inside her breasts even now, a literary mantra spoken in time to her heart's rhythm.

"No. No clue." Kieron's eyes shifted to the stage.

"It was my favorite. *Do not go gentle into that good night. Rage, rage against the dying of the light.*"

Kieron signaled the waiter. "Night?"

"Night's a symbol for death. Get it? Oh, never mind." Roxy threw her hands up in mock annoyance. She replenished her mug from the tiny teapot on the table.

Kieron looked back at her. "So?"

"I'm in, but you've got to promise no coat hangers."

Roxy knew the seriousness of the plan, but she felt exhausted. The memory of Thomas's poem had relit a wick within her, a reminder about the value of not giving up. Still, the idea that she would have to go the Anderson Clinic meant she may come out on a slab. What had she told Kieron? She was going to die anyway.

Roxy sat up straight. "Look, the Anderson Clinic is known for butchering people. Experiments—"

"Rumored and alleged."

"But, I'm dying anyway. Right? What do I have to lose?" Roxy said.

"So, tomorrow then?" Kieron asked and sipped her cocoa, trying to keep the anxiety out of her voice. Roxy could see her bouncing knee just outside the tabletop. Obviously, she didn't feel comfortable with any of this.

Roxy didn't like it either, but when currency was short, so were the options. "I've got work. So it would have to be Friday." Three days to get her mind right before going to the clinic.

"Great." Kieron blew out a sigh of relief.

Roxy wished she felt the same way.

* * *

Later, in her apartment, Roxy recalled how before the Great War, her grandmomma talked about the age of plenty. Healthcare for all. A united country. Not the puzzle pieces and scrambles for power the governors did now. Far below her window, streetlights glowed against the velvety dark. She curled up beneath her blanket with Tom-tom, her cat, complaining about the movement.

"Close program." As she turned to the window and adjusted the warm bundle of Tom-tom, her telemonitor blared. Her uncle's face consumed the left screen. The right side identified him as Malcolm Moore. With her father locked away in The District's cradle, and her momma vanished into the territory's seedy underbelly, Malcolm, her momma's brother, had taken an interest. He worked for the e-news violation section of the *D.C. Mirror.* He'd helped her get some jobs before helping himself to her currency. "A finder's fee," he called it.

Sighing, she answered the telemonitor. "Hello."

Malcolm's crystal-brown eyes peeked out from a pile of arrow-straight raven hair. A smile graced his lips and that usually meant trouble. He was all cheekbones, coolness, and cleverness. Or, so he thought.

"Oh, baby girl. Good evening."

Roxy stroked Tom-tom, who rolled over onto his back to give her better access.

"I'm calling to check in." He placed a cigarette into his mouth.

"I know."

"How did the doctor's visit go?"

Roxy's heart skipped. For the better part of two hours, she'd almost forgotten.

"Doctor Wu confirmed."

"What?" his voice cracked.

Roxy just sighed, unable to repeat it. "Don't wear that face to my funeral."

Malcolm mopped his face with his hand and regained his composure. If the situation hadn't been so sad, she would've laughed at her usually unflappable uncle.

"So, um, I guess the Baz Taylor treatment then?" He adjusted his cable knit sweater and repositioned himself. He dramatically tossed his shiny hair over his shoulders.

Roxy snorted. He couldn't be serious. "Sure. If you have the currency for it."

Malcolm drummed his fingers along the counter. "I'm not the man you think I am, niecey."

"Few are." Roxy glanced down at Tom-tom. "But, you're super reliable. Aren't you, Tom-tom?"

She kissed his fuzzy head and got an annoyed yowl in response. When she looked back at the telemonitor, Malcolm's face had returned to its usual polished on visage.

"The Anderson Clinic over on F or E Street offers it."

"So, I hear."

"Rox, go to the clinic. The Baz Taylor treatment can eradicate it. You can live. There won't be a funeral."

Roxy glared at him. "Currency counts, especially in healthcare."

"I wish I had it." He dropped his gaze. His performance almost seemed believable.

Roxy shrugged. "Sure."

"I'm really very sorry."

Roxy terminated the telemonitor feed. There were only two things she hated: robots and liars.

* * *

After work, Roxy arrived home with her body reeling and her feet barking. Once she fed Tom-tom, she set about unplugging her electronics, the telemonitor, the customized hologram program, and speakers. Before long, the door announced she had a visitor.

"Who is it?" Roxy asked, still dressed in her uniform.

"Terrance."

Terrance lived two apartments down. When she opened the door, he paused, looming over her like an ancient oak tree. His brown limbs, long and weathered, waved in greeting.

"I saw your post about the telemonitor, hologram, and speakers. That's pretty much your entire entertainment system. Right?"

"Yeah, come on in," Roxy said and moved to allow the tall man entry.

Terrance ducked his head. "Good price."

"You're getting them for a steal." Roxy gestured for him to follow her to the main room. *And a piece of my heart.* Her mother's gift, the telemonitor, and Kieron's gift, the hologram machine, meant a lot to her.

Terrance took in the system and whistled low. "You aren't lying. You sure you wanna part with these?"

Roxy shuffled her feet. "I, I'm sure." Not really. Her only certainty resided in the fact she needed currency.

Terrance took out his tablet and with a few swipes of his finger transferred the payment to her account. She watched on her cellphone as her balance increased.

"Thank you."

Terrance nodded and busily disconnected the telemonitor and attachments. "Nah, thank you!"

After he left, Roxy took in the empty apartment. She hadn't completely gutted it. Furniture, clothes, and books remained. All the things that could be sold had been. Their sacrifices accumulated in her bank account and shamed soul. Disbelief stained her vision. It had come down to this.

The only technology remaining, her cell phone, dinged. Great. A reminder of her appointment at the plasma center in 15 minutes. Roxy pulled on her coat and scarf, grabbed her wallet and headed out into the twilight.

Time to sell more of herself.

* * *

Friday came too fast. Roxy sat in her bed with the alarm blaring and Tom-tom pooled in her lap. Covers carved out a pocket of warmth around the cat. The gray, cold morning held hints of more icy rain, but the weeping welled inside of her, not from clouds. She would not go gently. When she climbed out of the bed, she realized that everything seemed brilliant, vivid, more colorful.

Could this be her last day on Earth? Is that the way it felt to everyone? Was her brain illuminating everything to log in her memory?

She showered.

Suds slipped down to the drain, like people who slogged through the bottom rafters of life— working, fending for resources, and then fading into some dark abyss.

Forgotten.

Somber thoughts for somber action.

This Doctor Mayes claimed he'd heal her with his version of Baz. Still, she wondered if the cheaper version was the same generic brand but with watered down effectiveness. Black market didn't come with a guarantee.

One could dream. The Internet's back channel lit up one night about the real cost of healthcare. How the poor paved the way for real medical research. How they were given experimental treatments— all Tuskegee like. When all they wanted was to be free of pain, of disease, and of death. What they often got was much worse than what they walked in the door with.

"Now, I'm one of those, Tom-tom. Among the medical lottery," Roxy said with weariness blanketing her. Still, she wanted to live, and to do so, she had to push on.

"*Rage against the dying of the light.*" She toweled off quickly in the chilly air.

Tom-Tom meowed.

She bent down and kissed him. "I will be back. Promise."

The real fear of not dying, but coming back not whole, took root. What if her cancer had been cured, but the doctor nicked an artery or the nanos altered her DNA?

The door rang and she snatched on her boots.

"Coming!"

Roxy found Kieron bundled in her favorite coat, but dressed in sophisticated clothes for the weather. The red scarf highlighted her hair's cinnamon streaks.

"I'm not going to ask if you're ready. I'm sure you're not," Kieron said.

Roxy put on her coat. "As I'll ever be."

Her stomach knotted as she patted Tom-tom and they left. Beside her, Kieron remained uncharacteristically quiet.

They took the elevator down and, once the metallic doors hissed open, stepped out on the sidewalk. A wind whipped through the morning, forcing them to walk closer together as a human barrier. The more it blew, the colder Roxy became. How much of her shivering came from the weather and how much came from the fear gnawing at the base of her heart, right beside her cancer— she imagined— she didn't know.

Kieron threaded her arm around Roxy's and pulled her close. "Let's get this done. We have passes to the Basin's big bash tomorrow."

Roxy quirked an eyebrow. "Tomorrow? Kei, I won't be recovered by then."

Kieron grinned. "Well, at least you won't be dead."

All too soon, they arrived at the Anderson Clinic. The flickering neon sign of the former pizza place next door seemed on the edge of fading, but blinked as if sending a frantic coded message before falling dark for good.

The automatic doors yawned open as the odor bowled her over. Despite its outward appearance, inside the clinic, state of the art technology and holographic informational doctors illuminated one corner and gave medical advice. The tile flooring was a warm mixture of ivory and black, and the walls held naturalistic art that changed every few minutes.

The people in the lobby didn't stir as they entered. Roxy's heart pinched at the despair and outright desperation weighing on them. Against the polished, professional, and gleaming clinic interior, the people within it— the sick, the injured, and the dying— were like faded flowers in a crystal vase.

The clinic had the reputation for using people as guinea pigs. Primarily by people hurt by their experiments, all in the name of scientific research.

Allegedly.

"Oh!" Kieron said and covered her nose. "It smells like bleach and ammonia had kids in here and then took them to the forest."

Roxy chuckled. The clinic smelled like most hospitals, except for the air fresher. In the center of the two automated glass doors Roxy could not move. *Now. Now's the time.*

The automated voice complained. "The door is ajar. The door is ajar."

"No, I can't do this." Roxy spun on her heel and turned to go back down the stairs.

Kieron stepped forward and grabbed her arm. "Come on. We're here." They walked in. Roxy couldn't promise she wouldn't walk out. She'd leave in a floating black corpse canister. They'd haul it down to the morgue and shove her into the insinuator. Those canisters were designed to burn— hot.

"Radiation tablets look real good right now," Roxy whispered.

"They probably smell better too," Kieron said.

"What's your name?" a bear of a woman inquired without looking over her screen. A wheezing rattled at the end of her words, and a sheen of sweat covered her face, making her makeup look wet.

"Williams. Roxy." Roxy shoved her hands into her pockets— too scared the woman would see her hands shaking.

The woman's lips moved as she read. "Ah. Okay. Taylor treatment." She shifted her bulk a little and gave Roxy the once over. "You've come to the right place."

"Can we get this over with?" Kieron said.

The woman squinted again at Kieron, but picked up her bright and shiny scanner. "Payment?"

Kieron thrust out her wrist. "Just take the damn currency."

The woman grinned as if it pained her, and ran the scanner over Kieron's arm.

"There's still a balance," the massive woman said to Roxy, smiling with a broad, tacked on grin. "Ma'am?"

Roxy fought to breathe and took to slow sips of air. At this rate, she would pass out before reaching the exam room. She extended her arm to the receptionist. Roxy prayed it wouldn't cost her life.

"Have a seat. We'll call you back in a bit."

"Thanks." Roxy lowered her arm and let Kieron guide her to the windows closest to the back of the lobby.

She turned Roxy to face her. "Don't worry. This is going to go fine."

Roxy held her gaze. "This place…"

"*Rage against the dying of the light. Do not go gently into that good night,*" Kieron recited.

Roxy smiled. "So you *do* remember it."

Kieron nodded. "So come on. I need you to rage against your *fear*, this place, the uncertainty. You did it."

"If it fails, or if somehow this makes the cancer accelerate—"

"Then we try the tablets, and then surgery…we will rage until there is no more of us."

"Or your currency."

Kieron laughed. "I have moms. They're doing well right now, so…"

"The tablets are like swallowing poison. The vomiting. The loss of hair…" Roxy shook her head. "I'd end up looking like a corpse anyway."

Kieron hugged her. "You'd be a gorgeous one, with or without hair. Though I prefer your locs— and breathing."

Roxy laid her head against Kieron's shoulder. It felt good to have someone who could reignite her spark. How could she have gone through any of this without Kieron?

The looming, unknown dark lay just behind the metallic doors that led to the examination rooms. She would rage against the dying of the light now that her own torch had been lit.

"Roxy Williams," the receptionist said, but didn't look away from her screen.

"Now?"

Kieron stood and shot Roxy a small smile.

Roxy released a deep sigh. A calm settled upon her. She would not be afraid of the dark, for she had a beacon in which to illuminate the difficult path ahead.

Sirens

Destine Carrington

The story of sirens,
people tell it well,
but they only know of ocean sirens,
not sirens of the well,

sirens of the pond
sirens of the swamp
unmarked vines and plantation rot

there aren't any waves
to brave
but kinks and curls
and a screeching hymn
flung from the fields
which gives these women,
provides, yields
the hearts of men
who sold their children.

The Conjurer's New Gospel

Kristian Astre

I have seen the goddess rise
— I cannot deny her —

from crystal shards and glitter tears

shimmering like a mermaid's tale

like pearls sweating in the sun

when she remembered where the treasure was

where the jewels had been hidden

there were no rubies, no emeralds, no gems

just the pulsing of her sacred sovereignty

midnight medicine thicker than molasses

running down her legs and into the earth.

Oh, I have seen the goddess

— are you saying you have not? —

swaying with ancestor secrets

a tranquil trance

pleasure-stunned with peace

blanketed in bliss

being fed puffs of cotton candy clouds

marinated in rays from the sun

sweetened by legions of high prayers

ascending in divine waves from an aqueous planet.

I have seen the goddess rise

— I can never unsee her now —

with the zephyr of her knowing

blowing brilliantly

never interrupting the dandelion fluff

that dares its tender self

to lean into the breeze to hear her

song of understanding

I have seen the goddess rise

and make the leaves her harp

plucking staccato bird notes at dawn

exhaling peach and mango juice sighs

into a cotton-mouthed sky

winking at the fading moon

as she invites the day to greet her

so life can begin.

Contributors

Stephanie Andrea Allen, Ph.D., is a native southerner, writer, scholar, and educator. She is a Postdoctoral Fellow and Visiting Assistant Professor of Gender Studies at IU-Bloomington, co-directs a literary non-profit for Black women writers, and is publisher and editor-in-chief at BLF Press. Her work can be found in *Lez Talk: A Collection of Black Lesbian Short Fiction, Sinister Wisdom*, and in her debut collection of short stories and essays, *A Failure to Communicate.* She is also co-editor of *Solace: Writing, Refuge, and LGBTQ Women of Color*, and *Black From the Future: A Collection of Black Speculative Writing* (Forthcoming 2019). She is a Hurston/Wright Foundation Workshop Alum. Stephanie is currently working on a collection of Black speculative short fiction and her first novel.

Kristian Astre's work has appeared in *Cannabis Now Magazine*, Merryjane.com, the *San Francisco Chronicle, 7x7*, the *East Bay Express, Revelist, Naturally Curly, Plenitude Magazine, Girls Get Busy*, and *SOMA Magazine.*

K.E. Bell is an undergraduate student from Baltimore who writes about black and queer feelings. Her writing has appeared in *Arsenika, witch craft mag, Cosmonauts Avenue, Vagabond City*, and *Efniks*.

Destine Carrington is a queer, Black woman living in North Carolina because she enjoys challenges. Other things she enjoys include but are not limited to: burgers, brownies, and Batman. Her work appears in *Drunk Monkeys Literary Magazine* and *Five2One Literary Magazine*.

Kivel Carson is an emerging writer concerned with social justice, inclusion, and representation through art and storytelling, particularly literary fiction and Afrofuturism. Her work examines human relationships, identity, and the unique ways in which Black women experience the world around them. She has worked in distressed communities of color in the rural south as a writer and community development coordinator. Carson has published both creative non-fiction as a journalist and fiction in print and digital media, including in the Caribbean literary magazine *Moko*. She has also won NC Press Association Awards for storytelling and investigative reporting.

Lauren Cherelle uses her time and talents to traverse imaginary and professional worlds. She is an independent publishing consultant and editor with a BFA in graphic design and MBA from the University of Tennessee, and writing certifications from the University of Louisville. She recently co-published an IGI Global book chapter about Black feminist treatment for sexual trauma survivors. In 2016, Lauren co-founded a literary collective for Black lesbian and queer women of color. Her co-edited projects include *Solace: Writing, Refuge, and LGBTQ Women of Color* and *Lez Talk: A Collection of Black Lesbian*

Short Fiction. You can find her southern/Black characters in *Lez Talk, The Dawn of Nia* (Resolute Publishing, 2016), and *G.R.I.T.S: Girls Raised in the South — An Anthology of Queer Womyn's Voices & Their Allies* (Freeverse Publishing, 2013).

Morgan Christie's work has appeared in *Room, Aethlon, Moko, Obra/Artifact, Blackberry*, as well as elsewhere, and has been nominated for a Pushcart Prize. Her poetry chapbook, *Variations on a Lobster's Tale*, was the winner of the 2017 Alexander Posey Chapbook Prize (University of Central Oklahoma Press, 2018) and her second poetry chapbook, *Sterling*, is due out this spring (WordTech Communications, 2019). She is the winner of the 2018 Likely Red Fiction Chapbook contest, where her collection *When Dog Speaks* will also be published in 2019.

M. Shelly Conner, Ph.D is an Assistant Professor of creative writing at the University of Central Arkansas. She is a multi-genre writer whose work has been published and/or produced by various publications and venues including: *Obsidian Journal of Literature and Art of the African Diaspora*; *Crisis Magazine*; *Playboy*; *The Root*; Black Ensemble Theater; Second City Training Center (Chicago); and *Solace: Writing, Refuge and LGBTQ Women of Color*. Shelly is also: the curator of the DapperVista lifestyle blog dappervista.com; founder of Quare Square Collective, Inc., nonprofit for queer artists of color; and creator of Quare Life, a web series that debuted at the DuSable Museum of African American History and has screened at Outfest and NewFest: NY's LGBT Film Festival. Her debut novel *everyman* is forthcoming (Blackstone Publishing).

Stefani Cox is a speculative fiction writer and poet based in Los Angeles. Her work has been published to *LeVar Burton Reads*, *PodCastle*, *FIYAH*, and the *Glass and Gardens:*

Solarpunk Summers anthology, among other outlets. She has received fellowships to Hedgebrook and VONA/Voices, and has previously served as an editor at *PodCastle*. Find her on Twitter @stefanicox or her website stefanicox.com.

Jewelle Gomez (Cape Verdean/Ioway/Wampanoag) is a writer and activist and author of the double Lambda Award-winning novel, *The Gilda Stories* from Firebrand Books. Her adaptation of the book for the stage, *"Bones & Ash: A Gilda Story,"* was performed by the Urban Bush Women company in 13 U.S. cities.

Her fiction, essays, criticism and poetry have appeared in numerous periodicals. Among them: *The San Francisco Chronicle, The New York Times, The Village Voice; Ms.* magazine, *ESSENCE Magazine, The Advocate, Callaloo* and *Black Scholar.* Her work has appeared in such anthologies as *Home Girls, Reading Black Reading Feminist, Dark Matter,* and the *Oxford World Treasury Of Love Stories.*

Formerly the executive director of the Poetry Center and the American Poetry Archives at San Francisco State University, she has also worked in philanthropy for many years. She is the former director of the Literature program at the New York State Council on the Arts and the director of Cultural Equity Grants for the San Francisco Arts Commission. She is also the former Director of Grants and Community Initiatives for Horizons Foundation, as well as the former President of the San Francisco Public Library Commission. She is currently Playwright in Residence at New Conservatory Theatre Center.

Leila Green is a writer from Milwaukee, WI. Her stories and essays have been published in *Electric Literature, Columbia Journal, The Offing,* and elsewhere. Her book reviews can be found on Instagram at @black.book.quotes. She is currently pursuing her MFA in Creative Writing at Syracuse University and is at work on her first novel.

Tyhitia Green writes horror, fantasy, and science fiction; although she sometimes dabbles in other genres. She began writing poetry as a child and ventured into fiction years later. Her work has appeared in *Necrotic Tissue*, *Nightmare*, and *Lightspeed* magazines. She is hard at work on the first novel in her dark fantasy series. She can be reached at tyhitiagreen.com.

Vernita Hall is the author of *Where William Walked: Poems About Philadelphia and Its People of Color*, winner of the Willow Books Grand Prize for Poetry and of the Robert Creeley Prize from Marsh Hawk Press and *The Hitchhiking Robot Learns About Philadelphians*, and winner of the Moonstone (Press) Chapbook Contest. Poems and essays have appeared in numerous journals, including *African American Review*, *American Literary Review*, *Atlanta Review*, *Mezzo Cammin;* and anthologies, including *Forgotten Women* (Grayson Books), *Not Our President* (Third World Press), *Dear America: Reflections on Race* (Geeky Press), *Unlocking the Word: An Anthology of Found Poetry* (Lamar University Press), and *Collateral Damage* (*Pirene's Fountain*). With fellowships and residencies from the Fine Arts Work Center, Ucross, and VCCA, Hall holds an MFA in Creative Writing from Rosemont College and serves on the poetry review board of *Philadelphia Stories*.

LaToya Hankins is the author of *SBF Seeking* and *K-Rho: The Sweet Taste of Sisterhood*. She has contributed to various anthologies including, *Don't Ask, Don't Tell, Lez Talk: A Collection of Black Lesbian Short Fiction*, and *REThink*. Hankins served as a judge for the 28th Annual Lambda

Literary Awards in 2016 for the category of Lesbian Erotica. She also writes a monthly column entitled "Hot Tea and Ice" at wyattevans.com/guest-writers/ and provides book reviews for the Black Lesbian Literary Collective at blacklesbianliterary collective.org.

She is a native of North Carolina and currently resides in Durham, NC along with her partner and three pets.

Maya Hughley is a passionate reader, writer, and procrastinator. She has a degree in marketing from the University of Texas at Austin and has written various pieces of fictions and poetry with varying levels of success. You can find her at mayahughley. com or in person attempting to finish a novel.

Nicole Givens Kurtz's short stories have appeared in over 25 anthologies of science fiction, fantasy, and horror. Her novels have been finalists for the EPPIEs, Dream Realm, and Fresh Voices in science fiction awards. Her work has appeared in *Stoker Finalist*, *Sycorax's Daughters*, *Baen's Straight Outta Tombstone*, and Onyx Path's *The Endless Ages Anthology*. Visit Nicole's other worlds online at *Other Worlds Pulp*, www. nicolegivenskurtz.com.

Radha X Riley is a multi-media artist whose work spans from spoken word and written prose, to philosophy and astrological readings, to visual art and instructional videos. They center the Black Trans experience in all of their work and hope to create a platform for QTBIPOC to tell their stories on their own terms. Their work has been published in *Beltway Quarterly*, and they are currently working on their first printed collection of poetry.

A regular at Spit Dat, DC's longest running open mic, they have featured at Washington Performing Art's District Vox, as well as the Congress Heights Arts and Cultural Center for Art All Night. They are currently the winner of TribeFestDC's Tribe Tuesday Showcase. It is their hope that their art will not only bolster their own wellbeing, but that of their community and loved ones as well.

Almah LaVon Rice's work has appeared in numerous anthologies and magazines. Her creative nonfiction appeared in the anthology, *Queer Magic: Power Beyond Boundaries*. She is the second place winner of the 2017 Still I Rise grant for Black women writers, and the winning entry, "Bloodlust: A Lullaby," is forthcoming in *Footnote # 3: A Literary Journal of History*. She's at work on her first book, a speculative memoir. She can be reached at almahcreative.com.

Eden Royce is a Freshwater Geechee from Charleston, South Carolina, now living in the English countryside. Her work can be found in *Strange Horizons*, *Apex Magazine*, *Fiyah Literary Magazine of Black Speculative Fiction*, *Fireside Magazine*, *PodCastle*, and *PseudoPod*. Her middle-grade Southern Gothic historical novel *Tying the Devil's Shoestrings* will be published with Walden Pond Press in 2020. Find her at edenroyce.com and on Twitter @edenroyce.

Nicole D. Sconiers is an author and screenwriter hailing from the sunny jungle of Los Angeles. She holds an MFA in creative writing from Antioch University, where she began experimenting with womanist speculative fiction and horror. She is the author of *Escape from Beckyville: Tales of Race, Hair and Rage*. The short story collection has been taught at Purdue University, Antioch University, California State University Dominquez Hills, among other colleges. Her short story "Kim" was published in *Sycorax's Daughters*, the Bram Stoker award nominated anthology of Black women's horror.

Her writing has appeared in *Clutch* magazine, *Neon V* magazine, *The Absent Willow Review, Inglewoodland,* and other publications, and she penned several exclusives for DrPhil.com. Her short story "The Stiffening" appeared on an episode of NIGHTLIGHT, the black women's horror podcast, and she was a guest columnist for *Nightmare* magazine's "The H Word."